IN THE MIDDLE

New Writing from the Midlands

First published 2025 by Dahlia Books
ISBN 9781913624194

Copyright © Selection copyright © Dahlia Publishing 2025

Copyright of each piece lies with individual authors © 2025

The moral right of the authors has been asserted.

All rights reserved. No part of this publication may be reproduced, stored in or introduced into a retrieval system, or transmitted, in any form, or by any means (electronic, mechanical, photocopying, recording or otherwise) without the prior written permission of the publisher. Any person who does any unauthorized act in relation to this publication may be liable to criminal prosecution and civil claims for damages.

Printed and bound in the UK.

This book is sold subject to the condition that it shall not, by way of trade or otherwise, be lent, re-sold, hired out, or otherwise circulated without the publisher's prior consent in any form of binding or cover other than that in which it is published and without a similar condition including this condition being imposed on the subsequent purchaser.

A CIP catalogue record for this book is
available from The British Library

CONTENTS

About Middle Way Mentoring

Abida Akram ▪ a quartet of short stories   1

Jessica Bell ▪ Vigil   12

Hongwei Bao ▪ Reunion   19

Maritsa Grey ▪ small flies   32

Zara Masood ▪ Skin Deep   39

Ashok Patel ▪ Where the Peacock Lives   51

Nisha Patel ▪ The Fire at our Factory   63

Ioney Smallhorne ▪ a duo of short stories   74

Michelle Wales ▪ Jonathan Strong   84

Imani Wenham ▪ Beaches, Barbies and Bakeries   102

Dionne Whitter ▪ Towards Utopia   118

Lynsey Wild ▪ Nell Discovers:
Not All Pain's the Same   131

About Middle Way Mentoring

The Middle Way Mentoring Programme is a two-year professional development scheme for Black, Asian, Minority Ethnic writers based in the Midlands.

The second round of the scheme took place during 2023-2025. Writers received mentoring for a period of twelve months from an experienced writer, and participated in a series of masterclasses designed to develop the craft of writing. Mentors included Susmita Bhattacharya, Rebecca Burns, Elizabeth Chakrabarty, Elaine Chiew, Michael Donkor, Melissa Fu, Amanthi Harris, Sairish Hussain, Vaseem Khan, Ashley Hickson-Lovence, Leila Rasheed, Leone Ross, Alison Woodhouse, and Kerry Young.

During the second year, writers participated in a series of workshops and talks delivered by industry experts, received bespoke career coaching. They also began to focus on completing a portfolio of short stories to send out to prizes, literary journals and to put forward for the scheme's anthology.

The Middle Way Mentoring project is led by writer and publisher, Farhana Shaikh with the support of a number of partners, including Bookouture, Curve Theatre, Dahlia Books, Renaissance One, The Literary Consultancy, Words of Colour, Writing East Midlands, Writing West Midlands and funded by Arts Council England.

ABIDA AKRAM was born in Pakistan and was brought over to England by two strangers, her parents, when she was four. As a child living in Greater Manchester, she tried to write poetry and wanted to be a writer. However, it is only after retiring from a long career in local government and higher education, and having moved to Leicestershire, that she has had the time to write short stories, flash fiction, and poetry with some success. She is now finally pursuing her dream of becoming writer, proving it is never too late to follow your passion.

'My World' was written in a day in response to a prompt about the elements. The inspiration was feeling overwhelmed by the news on wars and disasters. 'The Price Of Gold' was developed with my mentor and the group. It's the age-old story of some women's experience in many cultures. 'God Lives in a Barrel in the Sky' was written from the perspective of a child. When I was very young, I loved fairy stories and I really did believe that God, an old man, lived in the sky in a barrel. I also thought of a Roosa as a barrel then and if I broke my fast accidently during Ramadan then the barrel door would open and God would tell me off. 'A Pakistani Journey' is a child's memory of arriving in England.

Abida was mentored by Susmita Bhattacharya.

My World

Fire

Many voices. Fire ants are having their lunch as they crawl up my arms and legs. There is no ceasefire, nor will there be. No aid will get through. Hot and cold.

Blue and purple mottled patterns snaking from the soles of my feet and up my calves. The electric bar heater is too hot. I don't move away. We red-headed people are told we have a temper and are feisty so why am so I silent. This withdrawal is a bitch. I curl up as if paper torched by the sun. My ashes swirl in the room as if sparking the voices into chilli red flakes.

Air

Oceans deep and the deepest of space, unexplored. So much unknown. I am vulnerable to the invisible. I am vulnerable to the empty space inside. A black hole, never to be filled. Scared, drowning, I can't catch a breath. I wish I could see you once more before I choke.

Water

70% water. You're kidding, right? More voices from the TV. Loud. I laugh. My thirst is constant. I am drowning in the shallows of little saliva. Floods everywhere. Homes washed away; cars overturned. Strong trees brought low, slumping over roads. My body tight, holding on, whilst my eyes ache, waterless.

Earth

Bodies in white shrouds, bodies under flags, bodies in coffins, bodies in mass graves. You take all the genocides in your stride, for you will be there when we are long gone. You will cough up our bones when you are good and ready.

The voices are louder. There are no walls. There is no peace for such as I. The voices are knocking loudly. They say they are saving me from burning, that it's all in my head. You do not want to touch the body.

The Price of Gold

At the bedroom window she found a few moments peace. Finally ready in her crimson and gold embroidered wedding outfit. She stared out and upwards, seeking escape. A wide sky, pale laundered blue, looking down the hill towards Beaumont Park. She loved it here, in Huddersfield, this, her parents' home, known as the Summer House on the hill, because of it being painted sky blue. Gated, floating like a cloud. Distinctive in aerial views, evidenced in the many photos framed and hung along the landing.

Her cousins called to her, she moved slowly, heavy with gold. Still, it lifted the colour of congealed blood of her Asian outfit, mother had said it made her look paler, of more value to her in-laws. She shivered despite the August afternoon heat.

After the tamasha of the wedding, settled in a small, terraced house in Halifax, marked by red and white fairy lights over the door and windows. She slowly freed herself from the heaviness of stiff cloth and gold. The jewellery laid carefully in red velvet and satin square boxes. The bed behind her with its strands of red carnations and marigolds curtaining the bed from ceiling to floor on three sides. Glimpses of red and pink rose petals strewn on a grey satin bedspread.

Claustrophobic in a room too small for such a large bed, she lingered at the dressing table remembering her parent's happiness today. Startling at the sudden knock at the door, her mother-in-law bustled in as she opened her mouth to say 'come in'.

Her mother-in-law held out her hands, 'I will look after the gold for you beti; I will put the sets in the safe. Okay.' With downcast eyes she handed the boxes over. At the door, the mother-in-law said 'he is coming soon'.

She sat on the bed, staring into space. Waiting, her fingers wrestled each other. The door opens and the groom walks in. Curry fat and drink splodges spoiling the cream silk and embroidery of his wedding clothes. Roughly he pulls apart the strands of flowers. 'What! You undressed without waiting for me. Why? It is my job to undress you on our wedding night!' He sways and slurs his words, shouting as if that would hide his drunkenness. He staggers as he undresses.

She looks down and straightens her hands. She lies stiffly on her back as he lies down, naked at her side. 'Let me see if I can find my name in the mendhi' his fingers caress the paisley dark brown patterns and swirls on her hands, lower arms, then her feet, ankles and lower legs. Completely missing his name in Hindi in the pattern on her right ankle. He also misses the name of her school love, her first love, written on her left ankle. The left for the past, the right for the future, she tells herself again. His hands move upwards slowly, his breathing quickens, his eyes half-closed. She shivers and tries hard not to breathe in his smell.

She wants to escape, be a kite. As he explores the mounds and crevices of her body. She flies up over the Yorkshire moors, over the green and brown, looking down at the steep

Vs of valleys, the dirty stones of the villages and towns, the cream of the beloved Yorkshire stone concealed. Flying from Halifax back home to Huddersfield, seeing the familiar square of the rugby pitch, with the complex of cinema and entertainment. The bowl containing the hospital, the Civic Centre, a big Tesco and the Town Hall, all ringed at the top by conifers. George Square and the beautiful pillared railway station with Harold Wilson walking away, caught in an ever-present wind, always in motion.

Cold harsh moonlight lightens the room, occasionally the more yellow or bright white glare of passing cars briefly sweep through the room, revealing him asleep, snoring loudly. Her on the edge of the bed nearest the window, the whites of her eyes gleaming. The tracks on her cheeks, like snail trails. Red marks and lines of blood on the bare skin of her upper arms, her upper thighs and the left side of her face revealed.

God Lives in a Barrel in the Sky

Whispered directions from Mother tickle my ear, a 'Go quick, run!' along with a push out the back door. I fly on a mix of excitement and fear. Breathing hard, I run so fast that terraced streets become a red-brick blur. Cars have colourful streamers as they streak by.

God, the old man with the long white beard is watching me. His home, a large wooden barrel, is visible in the sky today. Hatch open, he stares down at me. 'Please God, let him be there...Please let me find him...' I implore, gasping for breath, as my pony-tail bobs and swings. His expression does not change. God is so old that I think he cannot really hear or see. That's why he never speaks. I am too breathless to offer him something in return.

The Park Inn looms. Mother always curses it under her breath. 'This is where the Devil lives' she says. I reach for the long handles on tiptoes, but the tall, dark, wooden doors are too heavy. Stuck, I wonder if I'm not naughty enough to gain entry. Before I start panicking one door opens inwards to a dark cavern. A goblin, round and short with a red nose and cheeks appears. 'Are you wanting to come in flower?' he waves me through as he leaves.

Blue air swirls from pipes and cigarettes along with stale yeasty smell. My eyes dart around quickly. Tall elves with flat caps sit around small tables. Some stand proudly in the centre of the vast room. I can't see him, God's magic has failed, I am frozen in place. Blue tattooed and eyed, a big bald ogre appears from behind a half wall. He looks me over from behind a tall square counter. 'Are you looking for your Da?' he bellows. I nearly nod my head off. Relieved that he is a kind giant. 'He's in the bog, be out in a minute. Wait there.' He lumbers off to see to bottles behind the half wall. I wait, one foot twisting behind the other leg, taking tiny sips of the poisoned air.

A man comes through a door on the other side of the room. All twinkly eyes and smiles as he picks up a big heavy glass from the half wall. It's Father and I think he is drinking Lucozade. Strange, as he isn't sick. The kind blue giant nods in my direction. Father comes over, eyes now like flat stones with anger. 'What on earth are you doing here?' he barks. My voice low and trembly as I quickly answer 'Mum wants you home straight away. Grandma has come, something about grandpa...' He sighs, then says 'Go on then. Scarper. Tell her I'll be there soon.'

I leave on jelly legs. Looking up into the cloudless summer sky, I see God's barrel is still up there, but the hatch is now closed. Maybe God is sleeping or visiting another child. Still, I shout up 'Thank you God!

A Pakistani Journey

Bright, clear, clean light. Dry shiny heat. A loving Punjabi village gathering in the summer of 1965. Amok with colour, noise and perspiration. Goodbye and good luck conveyed through garlands of precious rupee notes. So much money just for me! Was it real? I looked up at another descending garland. Then the kisses, tears and palms roughly flattening my hair. Grandparents and so many aunties, uncles, cousins and some neighbours and friends, who all wanted to be part of the tamasha.

'Don't forget us now.'

'Send some sona; they say the streets there are paved with it!'

'Take care, its cold there!'

'Such a long way away...'

Fear seeps into me as we leave the ground, sitting in the belly of a metal bird to fly up to the bright hot sun. The first miracle.

***

Fog tendrils lingered as a damp grey light appears. I shake my head. There are shadows everywhere. Different shades of grey with lots of pale ghosts walking by. I clutch at the folds of my mother's soft black burka, wishing I could see her face. Terrified. Shivering, I wonder what 'Victoria' is. The pale ghosts turn to stare at us in this vast dirty space. I try and hide in the black folds behind mother, trembling in my thin pink and maroon shalwar kameez with just a small black woolen cardigan on top. The loud incomprehensible voice from the roof, bounced around again up there in the vast empty space. Was it God?

The three of us, a still black triangle in the middle of this cold place. A tall Asian man stops and speaks to mother in Punjabi. Mother makes us follow this stranger onto a train. It is very quiet on the train, unlike back home, so we whisper. Back home trains had people sat on the roof, hanging from the windows and doors with everyone laughing, joking, eating and drinking and trying to catch a cooling breeze. I sleep, leaning against mother, hoping I would wake up from this nightmare.

After a few hours, I am walking, behind everyone else, down a black tarmacked street with rows of red brick houses on each side. There is a cold damp rain falling as we walk into the grey flag-stoned yard at the back of the house, to the shed with the toilet. I cry in there, missing the comfort and gossip of gathering in the field where we went together to the toilet, to fertilise the field. Later, I heard mother asking the stranger, 'But where is the soil? Where is the garden you promised me?'

Had I done something naughty to make the world lose all its colours and seasons?

***

It's not until I am six years old that I find my voice standing at the window and learn my first word in English: snow. I go outside to witness this second miracle. This cold, soft, white something melts to clear, clean water on my hands and tongue. It furs on my eyelashes and like magic, gives me a white cap on my thick black hair. Laughing, I join in, in making a snowman and fighting with snow laddoos.

JESSICA BELL was born and currently lives in Derby. She read English at Oxford, and is working for a refugee charity. She writes literary fiction.

As I'm finding often happens with my writing, 'Vigil' is the culmination of lots of intriguing tidbits which I've since gathered in a very magpie-like way!

I first came across Charles Allston Collins's painting, 'Convent Thoughts', as an impressionable, pre-Raphaelite-loving teen. Combine this with a fascination with the Victorian Gothic, religious expression, Claire Keegan's novella, Small Things Like These - and one special trip to the Mary Potter Heritage Centre in nearby Notts - and voilà!

Jessica was mentored by Melissa Fu.

Vigil

The winter just gone had been hard. It had seemed as though the snow had come along and had filled in all of the little inroads which Agatha had wrought with the attorneys, clerks, and counsellors of Temple and Gray's Inn. And, somehow, the lusts of even her most devoted clients – the blacksmiths, the barbers, the army officers, the retailers, the Tallow-chandlers – had been snuffed out by the frigid air. At the age of twenty-four, and having always been selective, Agatha had few friends still in the game who could help her out. And she could not see anything to gain in venturing to forge connections with the younger generation – or, at least, this was not something that she cared to pursue.

So, it was, on some level, a relief when she could no longer afford to pay fourpence a night for a share of that bed by the window in that grotty common lodging house. Life seemed to her a series of ends and deaths. She was desperate to conclude this time of scarce food and shelter.

*

Agatha felt unburdened as she apologised for her past wrongdoing and expressed her desire to be reformed to the Sisters at the House of Mercy. With a bit of effort, during her interview at the convent, she discovered a sorrow for the sins she found herself describing committing – sins whose sheer breadth impressed her, as she conjured them up in the moment. But she did not linger on that point, and she welded her remorse to a yearning for transformation. Having then also passed the medical examination, Agatha admitted herself to the asylum, under a pure and empty sky that whispered of the inevitability of relentless tomorrows.

The rite of passage after admission was to have a bath, the symbolism of which was not lost on her. Almost as if to aid the process of change, the temperature of the water was hot so as to send her lightheaded, enabling the erosion of her will into something that was soft and pliant. Enabling the erasure of self. The fact that they had confiscated her muslin and silk gown and had replaced it with their shapeless teal smock uniform was just the pinnacle.

Though Agatha was determined not to give them the satisfaction of languishing in her baptismal bath water. Yes, there had been a time when she was teetering into adolescence and had been led astray by Mr. Taylor. That was until a guest preacher at his Calvinist church raised a zeal within him, brimming over, that would convince him to scour his house of her, to cast her out with neither reference nor respectability. Yes, when younger, she had squandered the days in which she had glimmered as unchartered territory to clients. But she thought ahead to when the weather would improve and she would be back on the streets, and how she now harnessed strategy, as deceitful as a shadow, to counterfeit passion and to withhold la petite mort for anything less than one pound one.

She was in her prime, even if this year was to be her last to bloom.

*

Half past five in the Chapel for an hour's meditation, Agatha was hemmed in shoulder-to-shoulder with Sophie and Maud on a pew several rows from the front of the altar. Sophie was fallen insofar as she had ordered some biscuits in her former employer's name, whilst Maud fell by being a feeble-minded alcoholic. The space was solely illuminated by the six candles in the candelabra either side of the monstrance, and by a shaft of light coming from the opening in the coffered ceiling dome. Agatha had excavated the eight pillars supporting the ceiling from the dimness, as well as the giltwood wall brackets and festoons of garlands on the coving. In flickering intervals, she could also make out the icon of the bloodied heart of Jesus, lacerated by thorns, on the altarpiece. Having exhausted what was ahead of her, she lifted up a Bible from the book rack of the pew in front. She opened it at random to the story of the woman caught in adultery, to whose accusers Jesus said, "He that is without sin among you, let him first cast a stone at her." Agatha was being taught reading, with writing and arithmetic, by the Sisters, and was able to make sense of the narrative, which she strained to make out on the page in the dark, although she had never before encountered it.

She looked up and saw that Sister Jude, a novice, had knelt directly in front of her before the altar. The Sister was pitiable, often bedbound with bouts of lung trouble that she professed the doctor had said would steal upon her as a thief in the night and be the death of her. But the idea that Sister Jude should cause penitents such as Sophie, Maud, and herself to feel shame over the decisions which they had made in order to survive now seemed unfair. That is, the idea that they must genuflect to Sister Jude, and allow her the right to call herself their second and better mother, when she harboured trespasses of her own - and cruelty at that.

Never one for open discussion, the silence imposed at all times in the House of Mercy did not stifle her spirit. Never one for outbursts, the lashings of solitary confinement and physical labour for fighting or swearing did not stifle her spirit. But, as a creature who lived and breathed liberty, between the corporate 'family worship' and mealtimes punctuated by bells, between the smothering, constant nearness to others and the ten hours of sewing per day that were demanded of her, Agatha found herself trapped within a sculptured living tomb.

The Sisters had taken to shaving the heads of the inmates at the House of Mercy who tried to escape before the end of their two years as a punishment. But the thought of being rendered bald - or being subjected to any other form of discipline - was not a deterrent to Agatha. She was not like her father in that way.

*

A couple of months into her time at the convent, there was a believable premonition of spring. The crocuses and daffodils were peeking at the base of the walled garden's greenhouse, and leaves were filling out the bare lime and birch tree silhouettes. The horde of crows that had convened on the parapet walls of the convent was at long last dispersing. One vigil, a couple of hours after lights out, Agatha got out of bed, and her focus passed over the chair with the two identical smocks draped over, next to the desk with the prayer books and missal. She put both of these smocks on top of her night dress and plucked her boots off the floor and also put them on.

She was padding straight ahead down the corridor to the bathroom opposite her dormitory, when her eye was drawn to a fissure of moonlight pouring in through a curtain gap to her right. Knowing that the light was coming from where the novices' sleeping quarters lay, she was prepared to dismiss it until - between her light treads - she became aware of laboured, shallow breathing.

In the way of some vague, primal impulse, she stole across to the light shaft and saw that the curtain had been twisted back by Sister Jude, who was slumped on the floor, with one hand clasped to her chest, and a sheen of perspiration across her forehead. Agatha was about to resume her plan to escape when this got muddied, as Sister Jude's weary gaze made the journey of meeting hers. And Agatha was unnerved by a moment of vulnerability.

Agatha stalled and cursed the dilemma she had found herself in: if she stayed to help Sister Jude, the novice could see that she was planning to escape, and so she would be dependent on her kindness to not to tell the Reverend Mother. Agatha was uneasy with the idea of being in debt to anybody, not least Sister Jude, who, as condescending and intrusive as she was, would revel in another opportunity to be overbearing. Yet, remembering the doctor's words which Sister Jude had echoed, if Agatha left her and she died, Agatha's conscience could not abide by it.

Resolute, Agatha made her way to the bathroom and inched open the window until it was waist-height, stepping with one foot on the low sill to enhance her exertion. Only, she then swooped back to the corridor. Her heart was thundering in her chest and her palms were sweating. Her fingers made their way towards her dry mouth, before she steadied herself with a few deep breaths. Agatha wrenched the bell used to signal canonical hours out of its hook on the wall and swung it until she could hear stirring. She let it thud to the floor, as she tumbled into the bathroom again, just as the Sisters and the penitents began shouting, clipping the door shut behind her. She slipped out of the open window, and carefully worked her way up the adjoining drainpipe to the roof with care, unsinged by the need to hurry. The tile slates were slick, and a light mist of rain was swirling, and Sister Jude was drooping, and maybe it was her death knell that was tolling. But dawn was inescapably going to happen.

HONGWEI BAO is a queer Chinese writer, translator and academic based in Nottingham. His work explores queer desire, Asian identity, diasporic positionality and transcultural intimacy. His writing has appeared in Cha: An Asian Literary Journal, Ink, Sweat & Tears, Shanghai Literary Review, The Anthropocene, The Covert Literary Magazine, The Hooghly Review, The Other Side of Hope, The Ponder Review, The Rialto, Variant Literature and Write On. His flash fiction 'A Postcard from Berlin' was a runner up for Plaza Prize for Micro Fiction in 2023, and the judge Carrie Etter described him as 'Another writer to watch!'

As a queer Chinese writer, I constantly feel the tension between my queer and Chinese identities. While queerness is often seen as individualised, Western and white, Chineseness is often imagined as collective, heteronormative and queer-unfriendly. The clash between languages, cultures and identities that I feel daily informs the short story 'Reunion'. This is a story about four young people's friendship, love, dreams and the pursuit for a happy and authentic life, set in contemporary China. It draws on my experience of growing up in China and living in the UK. The story was drafted with the help of Vicki Grut and Jonathan Pizarro and developed with my mentor Rebecca Burns, and was longlisted for Plaza Prize 2023. It is part of the queer Chinese short story collection I am working on.

Hongwei was mentored by Rebecca Burns.

Reunion

I'm running slightly late because of the rush-hour traffic. When I eventually find 火锅, a hotpot restaurant in downtown Beijing, I feel both relieved and nervous. I'm here to meet three old classmates, my best friends from university days. One of them was my first love. Although the four of us have kept in touch by email and on social media, this will be my first time to see them in person after ten years. I've been looking forward to this moment for several months since I booked my flight from London to Beijing. It still feels unreal when I'm physically here, after ten years of absence from the city.

The restaurant looks bigger and posher than I expected. I follow an elegantly dressed waitress in an embroidered traditional Chinese garment through some gilded and zigzagging corridors. I finally arrive in an elaborately decorated room with Chinese ink paintings hanging on the wall. There they are: my three old friends sitting around a large dinner table. In the middle is a big boiling pot evaporating steam gently into the air.

Seeing me coming, the three all rise to their feet. The two women, Mei and Ling, wave at me with a bright smile. A big, tall guy walks up, holds out his hand and takes mine. His grip is firm, and his smile measured. 'Welcome, old classmate, long time no see! You still look so young!'

This is meant to be a compliment, so I reply with good humour: 'So do you!' The sad truth is that we have all grown bigger and older. Mei wears heavy make-up and is dressed in a tailored business jacket, looking feminine and professional at the same time. Ling has a flannel shirt and a pair of black jeans; her short hair makes her look like a tomboy and a rock singer. Yu is dressed in a navy-blue business suit, his red necktie slightly undone at the top of a white shirt. I'm surprised to see that time has left the biggest mark on Yu, who has grown from a slim, athletic youth to a chubby man with a beer belly.

As a visitor from London to Beijing, I readily leave the task of ordering dishes to the three locals. The waiter appears swiftly when called and retreats quietly after taking the orders. Soon the table is filled with neatly arranged plates of lamb, beef, vegetables, tofu, mushroom and things I don't recognise. Piece by piece, we throw these items into the steaming hot soup. Soon the soup is boiling, emitting a spicy, herbal aroma. We then help ourselves to the cooked, flavoured meat and vegetable, fishing them out of the pot and into the blue porcelain sauce bowls in front of us. Using his chopsticks, Yu puts a few pieces of my favourite wood ear mushrooms into my bowl: 'Eat more! You look so thin. You must have been starving in England.'

I was. Living in England on a modest student stipend, eating out was often a luxury. I survived on bread, pasta, salad and fried rice, but my cooking skills aren't great. There are hotpot restaurants in London. Many of them are hugely expensive; in comparison they look like the poor relatives of this Beijing restaurant. In the dark, long winter evenings when it was not raining, I would walk alone along the quiet, narrow London streets, missing the hustle and bustle of Beijing: its broad boulevards, colourful neon lights, endless flows of people and traffic…

Soon we are reminiscing about the beer and lamb skewer nights from our university days – except we are drinking wine this time. The university days were the happiest time of my life. Coming from different parts of China, the four of us – nicknamed the 'gang of four' – ventured into the small alleys in central Beijing, discovering the city's hidden gems and half-buried secrets. We drank beer and ate lamb skewers at a night market off campus. We got so pissed that no taxi driver was willing to take us back to campus. We took turns attending lectures, so the rest of us could sleep in while one person's lecture notes would ensure that we all passed the exams. It was no coincidence that we all chose to study at the country's best school of journalism. We were ambitious students, aspiring to use our writing to change society. We often debated about news value and journalistic ethics, concluding that China needed independent, objective and unbiased news reporting, and that the censorship of Chinese media must end, immediately.

After graduation, I left Beijing and moved back to my hometown in North China. I worked as a teacher at a local school for a few years, until I went to England to study for a Master's and subsequently a PhD. But the other three have stayed in the city. Ling is a local, so she does not need to worry about a residence or a residence permit. Her family owns two apartments in the city; as the only child in the family, she legitimately occupied one of them after graduation. As non-locals, Yu and Mei had to pull strings to get a Beijing residence permit and work hard to afford the high rent in the city. But both have secured jobs now and they have bought their own apartments. As a government employee, Yu has access to affordable public housing allocated to civil servants. Mei has married a rich businessman, and they live in a gated middle-class neighbourhood near the city's Central Business District. Both Yu and Mei are married and have children, but Ling and I are still single. I'm lucky to have escaped from the marriage-family-children complex because I'm a student living outside China most of the time – 天高皇帝远 (The sky is high and the emperor's power is out of reach), as an ancient Chinese saying goes. Ling is not that lucky. At the age of 32, she is already seen as a 剩女, or 'left-over' woman whose suitability for marriage is seriously called into question by her parents' nagging and relatives' gossiping, but she doesn't seem to care much about them, which is very cool of her.

We treat wine like beer and have several rounds of toast: 干杯 to our reunion, to our university days, to Yu's upcoming promotion to the head of news and his bright future, to Mei's perfect marriage and their plan to purchase a holiday home in the countryside, to Ling's debut novel and her promising career as a bestselling writer. As a poor student struggling to finish a PhD in a foreign country, I have nothing to report. And yet I still get toasts for potentially producing a pathbreaking PhD thesis and subsequently securing a professorial job at one of the world's top universities. A beaming smile spreads on every intoxicated face; the topics of our conversation expand as the hot steam rises into the air.

'What are you working on?' I ask Ling, a freelance journalist writing for websites and social media, 'Another Boys' Love story?' I was referring to the type of romance and often fantasy stories about beautiful men falling in love with each other, a popular genre among young people in East Asia.

'Probably not,' Ling sighs, putting down her chopsticks. 'The current situation in China is not good for writers like me. Have you heard of the writer who was recently put into prison for selling Boys' Love stories? I'm lucky because I published my book before the new law came into effect, and also because I'm not as famous as her. But I need to be careful. No more such novels in the future!'

I recognise her reference immediately. It was a scandalous court case from a couple of months ago. The writer was sentenced to ten years in prison for disseminating pornography, and yet all she did was write and sell Boys' Love stories. After the 2008 Beijing Olympics, the Chinese government has tightened control over media and publications. Homoerotic contents such as Boys' Love were put under strict scrutiny. This also coincided with a nationwide crackdown on LGBTQ organisations and community events. Shanghai Pride, the biggest public LGBTQ event in China, was forced to close down after ten years of running.

'Sorry to hear about this,' Mei says. She is a journalist at 时尚, a fashion and lifestyle magazine generously showering urban residents with juicy gossip about celebrities. 'My editorial office has rejected all the queer-themed stories submitted to us in the last couple of years. These stories used to be very popular, and our readers loved them. But the topic has become a real taboo these days.'

'I don't understand why the government takes such a hard line towards freedom of speech.' It's my turn to sigh. 'What are they paranoid about?'

'You've lived in the West far too long and you have internalised the bourgeois ideas of individual freedom,' Yu speaks suddenly, in a rigid tone. Yu is now an editor at 党报, an influential state-owned newspaper, often referred to as the 'mouthpiece of the Party'. 'Our country is a socialist country, and our society is based on collectivist values instead of individualist values. Boys' Love stories are part of popular culture. They serve the interest of the market and commercial publishers. They do harm to young people's minds.' He pauses a little and then continues his speech: 'Just look at how young people and pop stars are dressed and behave today: Men don't look like men, and women don't look like women. If this situation continues without check, how can we have a strong nation, and how can our country be respected in the world?'

'What are you talking about?' The tomboyish Ling is the first one to respond. 'You're talking like a government official. Have you been brainwashed?'

'I'm saying this not because I work for a state media company,' Yu says seriously, as if reciting a speech. 'China's socialist journalism is different from Western liberal journalism. It should have social responsibility rather than simply cater to the consumer market. Boys' Love stories are not good for children and young people. They should be banned.'

'These are very empty and subjective statements. We need a more diverse and objective media environment!' Mei is quick to respond.

'Western media claim diversity and objectivity, but they are full of bias and hypocrisy,' Yu grabs his glass and empties it. 'Look at how they portray China! What's so diverse and objective about that?'

'That's no justification for censoring news and suppressing freedom of speech,' Mei retorts. 'In fact, your newspaper is the biggest liar in China. It conceals social problems and glorifies the government. It has no soul and no integrity, just like you!'

'At least I don't get filthy rich by selling sensational stuff and even creating disinformation.' Yu says sarcastically. 'Most entertainment news from your magazine is celebrity gossip and rumours, and some come from dodgy sources. Stop your paparazzi from hacking people's phones and peeping into people's privacy! What's ethical about that? If this is what you've learned from the West, how on earth do you have the guts to talk about integrity?'

Mei falls silent, so does everyone else. One can hear the hissing of the gas fire and the bubbling of the hot soup. Suddenly I have a familiar and yet strange feeling of *déjà vu* – 似曾相识 as it is called in Chinese. We had similar discussions in our university days, and perhaps even on one of those lamb skewer nights. Our journalism training primarily followed the principle of liberal pluralism, often referred to as Western journalism. At that time, Yu was already attracted to the principle of socialist journalism, otherwise called journalism with Chinese characteristics under a strong Party leadership. The three of us would all argue against and laugh at him. Back then we were merely having a theoretical debate. No one took it seriously and it was OK to laugh things off. We were students; all we had was passion and idealism. Ten years on, with a professional life working for different types of media has changed our lives and outlook irrevocably. Now we are in different positions of power. Our worldviews carry weight and have real-life consequences. We are like strangers to each other.

'I've got to go. My family's waiting.' Mei stands up, collecting her coat and handbag.

'Please don't,' Ling also stands up, putting her hand above Mei's. 'He doesn't mean it.'

Ling turns to Yu and urges him: 'Say sorry.'

After a few agonising seconds, Yu reluctantly says: 'Sorry.'

'Thank you, old classmate,' Mei says in a sarcastic tone. 'Shall I feel grateful? You've changed so much. I don't think I know you anymore.'

With these words, Mei walks out of the room.

'I've got to go too. It was nice to see you.' Ling gives me a quick hug. 'Take care and enjoy your stay in Beijing! Keep in touch!' She then walks out of the room without looking at Yu.

There I am, left with Yu, surrounded by the cloudy steam rising from the hotpot, not knowing what to do. Yu collapses in the chair, his head in his hands. 'I shouldn't have said it. I couldn't help it.'

I don't know if he's talking to me, or to himself. But he appears so vulnerable at that moment, and that triggers something in me. I lay my arm around his shoulders, his broad, strong shoulders. He doesn't resist. He's tall, a big man, and yet he leans his head against my torso, like a child. I can smell the tobacco on his shirt and the alcohol in his breath. I can feel his body temperature.

There's again the sense of *déjà vu*. While we were studying together, there was no individual bathroom in the dorm, so we had to go to a public bathhouse. It was much easier to have someone to rub your back with a sponge and then dry it with a towel than doing everything by oneself. In the shower, he touched my body, and I touched his. We could feel each other's stiffness. In the final year, during the winter break, neither he nor I went back to our parents for Chinese New Year. We stayed in the unheated, ice-cold dorm room. Our bodies kept each other warm. Everyone was busy in the last semester: writing dissertations, doing internships and applying for jobs. I wasn't sure if Ling and Mei noticed any change, but Yu and I kept our relationship a secret. We acted like two ordinary friends in public. After graduation, we lived in different cities; we exchanged a few emails in a coded language talking about our own lives, until one day Yu told me that he was going to marry a woman. This didn't surprise me because I knew he would from our past conversations. He was an ambitious person and always wanted to live a normal life and become somebody. He had come from the countryside and, as the only son of the family, all his family's hope was on him. I congratulated him and wished him happiness. Our life paths diverged, and we hadn't contacted each other since. I've had a few boyfriends, but as my first love, Yu has a special place in my heart.

I decide to break the silence: 'I'm staying at a hotel tonight. Do you want to come over?'

Yu looks at me gently, his eyes sparkling and his smile mischievous. That reminds me of the primary aim of my long-distance journey, after all the long queues and endless waiting, all the sleepless nights and drowsy days, all the longings and yearnings. Everything is worth it. I had been looking forward to today's reunion, not only to rekindle the 'gang of four' friendship, but also to see him. Him in particular.

Yu's smile only lasts a few seconds. It soon freezes and his eyes turn gloomy. 'You know I'm married. I've got a family.' He says wryly.

'I do.'

'I'm trying my best to be a good husband and father. That's my duty, in the same way I must perform my duty as editor of a state newspaper,' his voice is dry and his hand is still holding mine. 'I don't want to live a life in the dark, like a criminal or a social outcast. I want a normal and respectable life. I don't have a choice.'

'Everyone has a choice. I've made my choice to leave China.'

'Because you can.' He says bitterly. 'Now you're free to be openly gay. What benefit does that bring you?'

'Freedom.' I say, although I'm not quite sure what it means: free speech? freedom to be myself?

'What's good about being free and poor and living on the social margins?' Yu asks rhetorically.

Suddenly I feel the impulse to defend myself. Yes, I'm poor and don't have a job, but my life isn't a failure; all my choices are worth it! 'I know I can never become head of news at a major newspaper in the UK; I know being Chinese is a hated word in the world at the moment; I know I will always be an outsider, a foreigner, a minority, in the society I live in, but that was my choice.'

I'm surprised by what came out my mouth, my sudden burst of anger. I can see Yu drop his head. He's still in my arms.

'Everyone has a choice,' I repeat to myself. 'I wish you all the best for your life and career.'

'The same to you.'

I draw him to me more closely. I can hear his heartbeat.

At the restaurant reception, a young man dressed in a traditional Chinese garment politely informs us that two female guests have already paid the bill for all of us. We walk out of the restaurant. The cold air makes me shiver. The street is still full of cars and people, busy and noisy as ever. At the door, we politely shake hands and bid farewell, like business partners. We then part ways and head towards opposite directions, like strangers who don't know each other and who will never see each other again.

MARITSA GREY is a lesbian fiction and poetry writer, with a Creative Writing MA from Goldsmiths University. She ran a queer short story publication from March 2020-2022, for which she won the Project Phakama Young Artist Award in 2021. In 2023, she co-founded a queer artist collective, Moonbuns, and has most recently published poetry with *The Passionfruit Review*, released March 2025. She lives in Nottingham with her wife and best buds.

The piece is, at its core, a celebration of the aggressive wildness of sibling relationships. It's the place we learn how to fight and what it means to be a friend.

Maritsa was mentored by Kerry Young.

small flies

The bananas were black and squishy. Three of them, still attached at the stalks, icy from being pressed against the back of the fridge. Kaz stared. Her dad kept the kitchen rubber-gloves-and-bleach clean, ageing bananas would not be tolerated in his household.

And yet, here they were. Grotesque in their rebellion. He came to clean the fridge, and did not find them, and here they had festered, waiting for her.

There were small fruit flies lining the rubber seal around the door, wriggling over each other. She had an impulse to run her tongue over the flies, to crush them between her teeth and swallow hard, to take some of their rebellious nature and hold it inside of herself.

She shut the door, hot liquid rising in her throat.

The sun was still high in the sky, pouring in hot yolk yellow through the kitchen window. It was the only time she really felt comfortable at home. Mia was watching tv in the living room next door, her laugh, low and rumbling through the wall, so different from the high pitched, twittering one she used at the dinner table. Their parents wouldn't be home for a few hours so, for now, the space was theirs. Were all kids like this? Holding their breaths, waiting for the quiet hours in between school and the end of the work day to breathe out again.

She lay the blackened bananas on the kitchen countertop. They really were quite repulsive. She pressed into the skin of one and soft flesh bubbled out around her fingers.

Using the kitchen scissors, she cut the stems off. Sweet and warm, they smelled almost like fresh fudge. She squeezed the bananas out of their skins like toothpaste and dropped ingredients into a bowl without blinking; flour, salt, sugar, baking powder, cardamom pods crushed between her fingernails. She started mixing, dry powder blowing up into her face, and the banana heavy at the bottom of the bowl.

What she needed was a liquid. She added eggs, and a splash of milk. She was a machine, mixing hard, her arms burning. She was power and movement and strength.

'We have a mixer,' Mia said. She stood at the doorway of the kitchen, watching Kaz from a respectful distance.

'Don't need it. I'm a machine,' she laughed. Mia frowned and walked away, and Kaz ignored the pinch of embarrassment. People found her funny at school, but not at home. Never at home.

The mixture looked smooth, save a few small lumps, but Kaz was sure those would add a nice texture, and smelled pretty good. She poured her mixture into a bread tin, stood back, and surveyed her work. It still needed some pizazz.

She poured granulated sugar into a heavy bottomed saucepan and turned the heat up high, and stirred. The sugar clumped, then melted into a thick amber liquid. She added butter, the pan frothing up into hot and angry sugary bubbles.

She grit her teeth, let the sugar spit up onto her arms, and kept stirring until the butter had combined.

Standing back, she watched the mixture rise in the pan without her constant stirring. She found watching baking videos was soothing, perfect for the nights when she lay in bed but couldn't quite catch her breath, her head loud and buzzing with thoughts that moved too fast for her to catch. But doing it herself, with her own hands felt good. It hurt more than she expected. She pulled the saucepan off the heat, and let the mixture cool. There was a layer of burned caramel at the base, but it was something she had made from nothing, entirely her own.

Pouring the caramel onto the top of the banana bread, it felt complete. She placed the tin in the oven, and turned the temperature to around 200. She grabbed a spoon, and began eating the leftover caramel from the saucepan. She hesitated, and took a second spoon for Mia, just in case she did want some. Not that Kaz would care either way.

Mia sat on the floor of the living room, arms hugging her knees like she was trying to take up as little space as possible, back ramrod straight as she watched Tuca & Bertie. Kaz watched her for a few moments. Something ached inside her chest.

She sat down on the sofa, the plastic leather creaking slightly.

'Wan thom cawamel?' she asked Mia. She held the saucepan out and thrust the extra spoon she had brought at her. Mia twitched and shook her head. Her grip on the tv remote tightened ever so slightly.

Kaz held the thick caramel between her teeth and leaned close to her sister's face. She mixed it with her own milky saliva until it pooled between her lips and dribbled down her chin.

'You utter freak' Mia said, the corners of her lips forming a snarl, 'Don't, you'll spit on me- NO'

There existed a sound of terror that only Kaz could pull from her. An animal sound, it made her voice come out at once whiny, feral, and filled with hatred. This sound lived buried deep inside Mia, so deep that none of her Terribly Cool friends had ever heard it. Her friends got to know Mia's secrets, they'd swear they knew her better than anyone, but they would never know her terror. That was only for Kaz.

'Wath do you meath? Ith SO YUMMY,' Kaz said. She twisted her body to avoid a few of Mia's punches, giddy as small drops of sticky spit landed on her face and arms.

They tumbled from the sofa and hit the ground together. They breathed in unison. Her head rang and her arms were sour with bruises that would form in the shape of Mia's fists.

Mia reached for the saucepan as Kaz began wiping her spit from her sister's skin.

'I think you burned this,' Mia said.

'Dunno. Haven't you seen this episode already?'

'Dunno.' Mia shrugged. Kaz nodded.

They didn't notice their Dad's car pull into the driveway. The sound of Mia chewing caramel must have deafened her, she would never usually have missed that sound, and would have been halfway to her room before he had even gotten out of his car. He was opening the front door, stepping into the living room.

'The hell kind of crap are you watching, Mia?' he said, 'Sitting down here like some little child, in front the tv and rot your brain?'

He didn't like rotting things. Kaz imagined Mia's brain, sat black and heavy, turning sweet between her ears.

'I was just-' Mia started. Kaz flinched. He asked questions, but he didn't want answers, she should know that.

'Fuck sake girl, you think life is easy? You think we come all this way for you to take the opportunities we work to give you and throw it away?'

It was crazy how quickly the air could leave a room. How fast Mia, tall, infinitely cool Mia, could pale and shrink. He still spoke, but his eyes looked in two slightly different directions, white foam collecting at the sides of his mouth. She wondered if he was even listening to himself, or if he just liked the feeling of shouting. Maybe it rumbled in his chest and made him feel strong.

She thought of the black flies, hiding in the lining of the fridge, writhing and repulsive and alive. She rose, slowly, from the floor. She held Mia's arm firm, and pulled her up, too.

'You sit back down, or I'll buss' yuh rass. Kassandra, you go find something to occupy yourself,' he said.

He gave her an out, she could leave, she didn't have exams, she was still at a perfectly acceptable brain-rotting age. Her heart beat loudly in her ears. He could beat her. A beating from him wasn't like a beating from Mia. One was wild and feral and left her feeling happier than before, the other was calculated and calm and made to make her feel weak.

Kaz walked closer to her father and looked into his eyes. He had long lashes like hers, so long the ends would tangle together every time he blinked. He looked at her with an expression she didn't recognise. The top of her head came up to the middle of his stomach now, higher than it had ever reached before.

She could take her head and fling it like a weapon and press it deep into the soft meat of his belly. The thought came to her, crisp and clean and obvious. She felt Mia's palm sweating heavy against her own, and she knew that, if she struck their father in this moment, that her sister would ball her hands and punch and leave his skin burning with bruises.

She knew this with certainty and the thought made her smile, and something in their dad's face told her that he knew it, too. Something about the way he looked down at his feet as she walked past him. She was quite big, actually, and her sister even bigger, and they would continue getting bigger as he only grew older. She pulled Mia with her out of the house. The air outside smelled sweet and heavy, like banana bread about to burn.

ZARA MASOOD is a British- Pakistani artist and aspiring writer. As a recent graduate she is starting to embark in her creative journey and find her voice as a creative. Her go-to is poetry , and she's performed a few times, but Middle Way has given her the opportunity to delve into finding her voice through prose.

Her work mainly focuses on the lived experience of diaspora and identity. She is currently writing a story on alienation and post colonialism.

'Skin Deep' is a story that has shape-shifted from the moment of its conception. But was always about being a second-generation immigrant in a country that colonised your own. All those moments of 'Othering' all us Others go through. The tug-of-war between British and Other you feel. Of coloniser and colonised. I've struggled at times with the weight the story carries for me, the ugliness it has made me look at.

This story followed the murder of George Floyd and the global Black Lives Matter protests, while a virus attacked our bodies and hate spread. Far-right, anti-immigration racist riots broke out in the UK 2024. This is not a problem of the past. We can not pretend the 80s were the only time when racism was bad. This was not a story I wanted to write. But the more I wrote the more it became one I had to write.

Zara was mentored by Elaine Chiew.

Skin Deep

'Once upon a time – guys are you listening?' The children's mother asked sitting in front of their shared bunk bed. Zehr, the elder of the two, on the top, and Roshan snuggly tucked in the bottom. 'Zehr?'

'Yes mum' It replied.

The room was dimly lit with a small light that Roshan liked to sleep with. At first Zehr didn't like the light but then Mum bought one with a star pattern that would paint most of the ceiling. Zehr didn't mind so much then. Zehr stared at the ceiling.

'Roshan, you'd better be listening because Zehr let you choose the story.'

'And you chose the story of 'The Shedders' again. I don't know why you always chose this stupid one. It's sad,' Zehr chipped in annoyed at its sister's choice of bedtime story.

'I like it because it's scary. I like scary stories. You know, nani said she saw one when she was young. Her and some other girls would feed it. Leave the food outside the cave. Then one day when she was a teenager, she waited for the Chilke Wala to come out and hid behind a bush. She said it was the ugliest thing she'd ever seen. Even in its dirty old robe covering it, its arm looked like it had been melted in acid. And his face, like something had chewed it and spit it out. She screamed and ran away when it looked at her. It came after her, but it couldn't move as fast.' Roshan recalled from her grandmother.

'Of course, nani would say that.' Scoffed Zehr. Not pointing out how ironic it was that Roshan wanted a scary story when she still needed a nightlight.

'What do you mean?'

'Maybe he was just trying to say thank you.'

'Monsters don't say thank you.'

'Is that what she called it? A monster' Zehr asked.

'Yeah.'

Zehr was quiet. The room was silent for a few heavy seconds. Their mum looking between her two children.

'It wasn't a monster. It was a person.' Zehr stated. Its feelings hurt, but it didn't know why. It just did. Empathy was always a big emotion for Zehr. Its mother always thought it would make Zehr a good healer. It could almost feel the sorrow this Shedder must've felt. The loneliness. Zehr knew a little bit about loneliness.

'The story's more fun if it is a monster. Anyway, she never went back.'

Just as Zehr was about to rebuttal, their mother interjected. 'That's enough you two. Nani made up loads of stories when I was little. Who knows if shedders are even real. They've always been a folktale. Even in Etiolatia.'

'I hope it is real. I want to see one someday.' Gleamed Roshan

'I hope it's not' Zehr whispered to itself, turning in bed, pulling the duvet over its shoulder. 'Nobody should be called a monster.'

'Everyone ready this time,' their mum asked. She was met with silence. 'Okay, so, once upon a time -'

The story was known as 'The myth of the Shedders,' The myth goes that …

'–There were these people. The Shedders. In Adustian they're called-'

'I know. The Chilke Waley.' Roshan added.

'That's right Roshan. These people were born normal people. But they didn't fit. They didn't know who they were. They asked questions. Their uncertainty made them question everything. So many questions that it drove them to madness causing them to only talk in questions.'

'That's one of my favourite parts. It's like talking in riddles.' Roshan chirped.

'Questions but never answers. In their madness they would isolate themselves or get shunned from civilised society, living in places where others wouldn't go.' Their mum told.

'Wait you're telling it wrong. This is the part where The Shedder get hunted by the locals.' Roshan said chiming in again.

'Nope. Not in my version. That's not how it goes.' Their mother replied doing her best to shut the conversation down.

'But mum—'

'If you want me to tell a story tonight, this is how it goes.' She had jumped a paragraph in the book intentionally. She too, did not like the story. Especially that part. Lifting her eyes from the pages, she checked Roshan was done talking for good and looked higher at Zehr, who was facing away from her and to the wall instead.

'They'd reside in the neglected spaces, caves, forests and dilapidated buildings. Driven by their madness they pick at their skin. It would come off in pieces. They healed and repeated again until they shed slabs of skin unconsciously and habitually. The rate of their shedding would increase from a few times a day to hundreds. Eventually the skin wouldn't even bond to the muscles it would stay loose and slide off until there was no skin left to shed. Skinless and homeless the shedders would whittle their days away shivering and muttering incoherent questions. It is rumoured that sometimes when it is quiet you can hear their whispers in the wind, 'Why…?', 'How…?', 'What…?', 'When…?', 'Who am I?' Nobody knows what happens to them after that or if they were even real, but people would use the story to scare children asking too many questions.'

'See Zehr? You shouldn't keep yapping on with your boring questions.' Teased Roshan, she couldn't help herself.

'Don't be mean Roshan or you'll be washing up for two weeks. Go to sleep now.' She said as she placed the book back on the cluttered shelf and left, closing the door.

Zehr didn't say anything and pretended to sleep. It looked up at the ceiling as it waited for it's mother to leave. In the shadows and forms of sculpted light created by the celestial nightlight, Zehr picked out shapes that were cast above it on the ceiling. Usually, it was a half-formed animal or a face, today it was a cave.

That night Zehr had a nightmare. It was trapped in a cave; it was cold and dark. It scrambled around for rocks to use as a flint and made a fire. A spark. Then another few spraying out erratically. And finally, a light. Except it wasn't the flame Zehr was expecting. Instead, it was the starry night light from its bedroom. Zehr awoke its body violently jolting as if struck by lightning. Its limbs felt heavy and buzzing. Zehr gulped at the air as it tried to settle back down. 'It was just a dream' was the only thought looping in Zehr's mind. Just a dream.

Zehr actively didn't follow in its nani's footsteps in its life but, whenever Zehr passed a cave, it would leave some food if it was carrying any, and a flower if there were some close by. With a note with just one word.

'Sorry'. Still hoping that shedders weren't real.

A FEW YEARS LATER…

Zehr was always a quiet kid. Until, it had a question. Then, there was no stopping the spillage of words out its mouth. Like, 'But mum why is the sky actually blue?', and 'Why can't we see Adustia during the day?'. Its mum explained about how the light from the sun is so bright it drowns out the reflection of light that made us see Adustia from Etiolatia. That's why Zehr loved the night so much. The dark. When everyone and everything hides away, Zehr, the moon and Adustia come out. Zehr would look up at Adustia every night. Sometimes for hours in the garden sat in a worn, discoloured lawn chair, thinking or not thinking, like a small ritualistic homage, looking up and mentally teleporting away. Or sometimes just a peek through the curtains saying goodnight. Zehr's ancestral home planet looked so small from here. Like an orange and gold speckled walnut floating in a deep vastness and backdrop of a hundred stars, looking its most beautiful on a full moon. The moonlight dancing on the surface of Adustia making it glow.

Its fondness for the night sky and all its adornments had Zehr turning to books. Trying to find all the answers to its question about the workings of the universe. About Adustia, Etiolatia and where it fit. It didn't find all the answers it was looking for in books however, just more questions. It did well at school. Really well. Top grades. Zehr liked the actual learning part of school.

Zehr's mum secretly applied for Zehr to have a scholarship to Starlight Academy. The school was a private school filled with snobby Etiolatians and a few even snobbier Adustians whose parents where mostly Neo—derms. Neo-derms were non-Etiolatians that undergo the process of melanin deletion using concentrated UV lasers. It would make them look more Etiolatian. For most off-worlders, that was the aim, to be Etiolatian. The school's motto was 'SHINE BRIGHT AND TAKE YOUR PLACE AMONGST THE STARS.' Despite its seemingly motivational message, it unconsciously alluded to the colonial endeavours of the school's alumni a few centuries ago. The scholarship only existed to show that it wasn't just a place for the rich and privileged. They'd get in a kid from the Pots- where Zehr was from, usually just one if they could help it. They often didn't last a year let alone the whole five. They'd make sure to get the Pots kids on the posters, in the background somewhere though. You know, filling their quota.

Zehr got in. It didn't want to go. It liked going to its school now, Unity, and the walks with Roshan in the morning and on the way home. Roshan had tons of friends that it could walk with but they always walked together. Mum said they had to. At first Roshan liked it, when it was its first year at school with all those people, having her older sibling there felt comforting. Roshan and Zehr were the closest in age, out of all three siblings. Only one and a half years apart. The youngest of the three was only four. Zehr was very protective of Roshan and never wanted anything bad to happen to her. When they were young, you'd find them together all the time. They would wake up, before the sun had risen, to watch the television really early in the morning, legs dangling off the sofa, holding bowls of cereal. Roshan would always spill a bit and Zehr would clean up before their mum came downstairs so they wouldn't get yelled at. Talking for hours at the end of the day in their bunk beds. They didn't mind not having any personal space when they were that little. Their lives were so intwined it didn't matter. But they would fight a lot too. At first it was small things, like who's turn it was to play with a toy. Roshan was the most important thing to Zehr. It would always favour Roshan over itself. Roshan did not do the same for Zehr. Often Roshan would take advantage of this and eventually Zehr didn't feel good being around Roshan and felt itself slowly withdraw from their relationship.

Over the few years though Roshan got herself some friends like Zehr always knew she would. Roshan was always much more outspoken and sociable than Zehr. The walks that were always filled with conversation were now saturated with a heavy silence. Zehr felt like a drain on Roshan, knowing that it didn't want to be there with it. But mum said. And Zehr was still glad for the time they got together.

The entry exam for Starlight was something children would study hundreds of hours for, with tutors and wet cheeks that led to childhood burn out. Zehr had a month. It passed. Barely.

'I know you're not keen on this school Zehr but you're lucky. Some kids work their whole life to be here. Don't waste it. Just try it, okay? For me.' Its mum said.

'For mum', Zehr repeated in its head as it shopped for its uniform in the all Etiolatian neighbourhood. The shopkeepers seemed shocked at their presence in her shop and looked at them as though they had invaded. She followed them closely and would look at them in disgust when it would talk its mother tongue with its mother. Zehr would often feel ashamed speaking Adustian in front of Etiolatians because of the looks and whispers. It rarely did now, slowly losing the language like many other Adustians in Etiolatia. The shopkeeper reluctantly handed them the clothes they asked for, standing as far as she could. Zehr got a size up so it could grow into it like it always did. Roshan hated doing that. Zehr quite liked it, the extra fabric helped it feel safer.

The gate was the first thing you were met with. Despite its beautiful craftmanship, in that moment it was the scariest thing Zehr had seen. Standing there in front of the wrought iron gate, Zehr felt like it was wilting. Zehr walked onto the ground of Starlight Academy, trailing behind its mother, tucked under her shadow; it hadn't done that since it was the height of its mother's knee. It was the same height as her now. The school itself dropped a shadowing presence over them, charged with stillness, as if you had walked into an abandoned house that hadn't been aired in years. Preserved and stagnant. Hundreds of years old, it was a monument to the era of 'Great Old Etiolatia'. The grass was so green it seemed like a high-definition hologram. The path that painted the way to the grand entrance was so straight, Zehr imagined someone crouched down on their knees cutting the grass lining it with a pair of scissors and a ruler. Growing up Zehr never thought they were well off, but walking on the grounds of the Academy, it realised just how true that was. Starlight was only a few miles away from Unity, but it was easy to believe it was a different planet. Zehr felt very far from the Pots.

From the moment it stepped foot in the school, clad in the stiff new uniform with its mum, Zehr hated it.

'Are you nervous?' Zehr's mum said glancing over her shoulder.

'I'm fine mum.' Zehr lied.

'It's okay if you're not. It's your first day.' Mum said trying to calm Zehr a little. They got to the entrance. 'I'll leave you here, okay. I don't want to embarrass you.' She said now facing Zehr, taking in what it looked like in its brand-new uniform. The clothing was so fresh Zehr thought it could stand up on its own without its body as a mannequin.

It was lunch. Finally. Zehr sat down at a table alone. Hoping to hide away from all the inspecting eyes. Being the new kid was not an experience Zehr enjoyed, it felt like it was in a zoo and it was the only animal. Wild, compared to the rest of the children at the school, at least that's what they all seemed to think about it. Opening its lunchbox Zehr started to eat yesterday's left over dhal chawal.

'God, that reeks. We should evacuate the whole canteen and quarantine it.' Zehr closed its lunchbox.

'I bet it would still smell after a week. Does your house smell? Guys do you think the new kids house smells?' Asked a girl that was clearly popular, judging by the number of other kids she had clustered around her. Some Adustian. Most Etiolatian.

'Yeah' they sang like a choir. They all looked identical.

'Even it smells.' Said one of them. Zehr noticed she was in its class earlier.

'It? What like the outer aliens?' Asked the girl at the front.

'That's how the new kid said the want to be called. 'It''.

'What's your name new kid?'

'Zehr.' It said without looking up and opening its lunchbox for a second time.

'What a Dusty.' Said the girl at the front. They all laughed and walked away. Zehr put its spoon down. It didn't have an appetite anymore. Zehr knew the word. Every Adustian living on Etiolatia knew the word. It had just never been called one before.

After that day, there were some days Zehr didn't eat any lunch, it didn't want to open its lunchbox. To be judged by the Etoilatians. Worst of all though was the mean Adustians. They would laugh too. They would say 'Why can't your mother just make Etiolatian food?' Zehr didn't know why they would say 'what a Dusty' when they thought Zehr couldn't hear. Zehr did hear. And felt betrayed. Zehr didn't have any Etiolatian or Adustian friends at Starlight. It was all alone. So, Zehr waited until everyone was done and the dinner supervisors weren't looking and throw its food away. And when its stomach rumbled Zehr used to think, 'at least I'm not a Dusty'.

ASHOK PATEL is a Lecturer in biomedical sciences and lives with his family in Birmingham. He has written a short play for stage which toured nationally (Jeevan Saathi; Life partner), two community plays (Multicultural and Ninety days) and a BBCR4 afternoon play (Jeevan Saathi; Life partner). He has had three short stories published (Ninety days in Dividing Lines, Milly in Five stories and Hotel Shalimar in Thursday Nights) and has written scripts for three short films which have been produced (Obsession, Chahana and Cathy and I).

Ashok was mentored by Vaseem Khan.

Where The Peacock Lives

PROLOGUE

The southwest monsoon was unusually late this year and everybody in Gujarat collectively held their breath while it languished over Kerela seemingly reluctant to move further north. The state government had ordered any available water to be rationed for people and their cattle. Farmers had sleepless nights waiting for the rains before they could start to seed their crops. Lord Varun must be particularly angry this year, they whispered, as they stared at their cracked and parched land.

With each passing rainless day people did their best to persuade Lord Varun to deliver the rains. Professors and students in MSU's Faculty of Arts cancelled classes and held a puja in the campus temple where they sang the Raag Malhaar. Fifty-five-year-old Pankaj Patel from Kandola, stood on one leg in a vat filled with water in a Swaminarayan temple in deep prayer for twelve straight hours. A tribal community in north Gujarat collected money from each family and made seventy kilos of ladoos and fed them to stray dogs. The rifts and divisions between castes and religions were put aside as they all came together as one and begged Lord Varun to bless them with life-giving water.

In a remote village in Maharashtra every family was devoted to Lord Shiva and each house had a small hollow space, a devasthanam, where cobras made their homes. The snakes were venerated, regularly fed with milk and eggs and roamed freely around the village, often basking in the sun near young children playing in the dirt. The villagers prayed fervently to Lord Shiva to end the drought and gave their cobras extra milk, eggs and water. Every day they lit divas and incense sticks in steel trays with kumkum and flowers, and sang artis passionately.

And the southwest monsoon did arrive finally.

Chapter one

Vinod wondered if he would ever get used to driving in India. He sat in his white Tata Safari hemmed in by other SUVs, cars, rickshaws and multi-coloured trucks and surrounded by a cacophony of blaring horns and raised voices. The traffic crawled along like a cornucopia of slugs. Passengers left their vehicles and returned with freshly cooked bhajias, paper plates crowded with pani puris, and ice-chilled bottles of Thumbs Up and Fanta from roadside vendors. Exhaust fumes embraced the smell of spicy food fried in the open air and lazily wafted into Vinod's car bypassing the closed windows. When the southwest monsoon had finally arrived two months earlier, people had danced for joy in the streets and villages, and the torrential rains had healed the cracked and parched land and tamed the fierce summer heat. The temperatures had risen steadily since and the temperatures outside his air-conditioned SUV reminded Vinod of the summers at their height back in the UK.

An old woman hobbled along the mayhem of vehicles, her back locked in a curve, begging for money with hands clasped. She wore a stained and tattered cotton saree with one end pulled over her head and was bare footed. A stone's throw away was a five-storey black glassed building bulging with call centres servicing the needs of multi-national companies around the world. When she approached Vinod's car, he lowered his window and slipped a note into her outstretched hands. A toothless smile spread across her face when she saw it was a hundred rupee note and she showered him with blessings as he shut his window quickly. She probably wasn't much older than him, Vinod thought, but looked much older. But then they have led very different lives. Though in his mid-sixties, he was still quite fit and active, and most people thought he looked younger. His hair had thinned and receded, and it was grey at the sides which, his wife said, made him look distinguished. He watched the old woman knocking on other cars in his wing mirror and sighed under the weight of his privileged karma; a feeling he only ever experienced in India.

The traffic started to move quicker and twenty minutes later the vehicles approached two cows sitting on the road chewing nonchalantly, oblivious to the chaos that they had caused. Both had kumkum and rice splattered foreheads. There was a reverential lull in the honking of horns and shouting as the traffic squeezed into single file and passed by them. Once past this bottleneck Vinod was soon on the highway to Sadlav, the village where his family had lived for generations and where he had grown up before moving to the UK in his early twenties. Now, over forty years later, the journey of twelve kilometres from the bustling town of Navsari to Sadlav was unrecognisable. Palm trees lined both sides of the newly built tarmac highway and beyond them were fields with crops of sugar cane, maize, cotton and rice. Dotted along this road were residential complexes with flats and houses for India's burgeoning middle classes. More complexes were continually being built and the value of the land adjacent to both sides was constantly rising. It had become common for people in villages to sell some, or all, of the land that had been handed down in their families for generations, to property constructors. They often used the money to modernise their ancestral homes in the villages or they sold up altogether and moved to houses in desirable locations in Navsari.

Vinod had been reluctant to sell his family home and land. Many generations of his family had lived in that house in Sadlav and survived off their crops of mangoes and sugar cane. For a few years his wife's younger cousin had cultivated the land and was allowed to keep the sugar cane that he grew. He harvested mangoes and pruned the mango trees regularly. But ill health forced him to stop working a few years ago and Vinod had not been able to find anyone reliable since. As he came off the highway and into Sadlav, he wondered if the time had finally come to sell up. He drove along the main road of the village and turned into a small lane. He parked outside a two-storey house with a veranda and a traditional mahogany door with a padlocked latch. All the windows were barred with wooden shutters inside and an upstairs balcony that ran along the length of the house.

Vinod and his wife Bhanu had bought a house in Navsari many years ago when they had lived in Leicester and their daughter Rekha was quite young. It was an investment, but they also used it on their visits to India. But then his wife developed diabetes in her late forties, and despite her best efforts, her heart and kidneys began to fade. She carried on working for another ten years and then took early retirement from her job working in a jeans factory. Without the focus of work, she found the English winters increasingly difficult, and Vinod noticed that her health worsened during those cold dark months. He made the difficult decision to retire from his job as legal clerk in a solicitor's office, a job that he had been in for thirty years, and they moved to India.

Their daughter Rekha had got a job as a biomedical scientist in a London teaching hospital quite soon after graduating from university. Their relationship had become distant over the years, but they lived in hope that it would improve. She wanted to settle in London, so they sold their house in Leicester and used half the money to help her buy her own flat in south London. Neither they nor Rekha were likely to want to live in Sadlav so there hadn't been much point in spending money on the family house.

He opened the padlock, pulled back the latch and pushed open the thick wooden doors releasing the dank and musty air inside. He went round the house and opened all the wooden shutters and let the light and fresh air in. Memories of his childhood flooded back. The tiny kitchen where he often sat cross-legged next to his mother as she cooked over an open fire. He remembered her throwing spices into bubbling pots of vegetables and letting him stir them occasionally. She made chapattis on a tawa and always gave him the first one, spread with ghee and pinched his cheek as he took a bite. The swing in the front veranda where he sat with his father in the evenings was still there. The evening breeze used to bring with it the chatter between the neighbours and the noise of the children playing. He used to run with the other kids along the dusty lane to the well at the end and gleefully watch the frogs jumping about at the bottom of the well. One of the rooms upstairs was always piled high with mangoes in season. He smiled as he remembered how he and his friends ate as many as they could before they were taken away and sold.

Vinod sighed. His house and land lay uncared for like a stray dog. The well had dried up long ago and the dusty lane was now tarmacked and crowded with motorbikes and cars.

'Everything's changed eh?'

Vinod turned round to see his elderly neighbour standing in the doorway of house next door. He had aged visibly since the last time he had seen him. He looked frail and leaned heavily on a walking stick. Vinod smiled and walked over to him and gently embraced him.

'Good to see you kaka,' Vinod said.

'Nobody has time to talk anymore,' the old man said pointing his stick at the surrounding houses. 'Everybody busy-busy. You haven't been here for a while?'

'Bhanu hasn't been too well, kaka and I've been busy with the Committee at Vishnu Society.'

'I know, I know. Everybody busy-busy,' the old man said.

'A constructor has asked to meet me here. He's interested in buying my land,' Vinod said.

'Ahh! I have seen people looking at your land.' The old man cackled open mouthed revealing the few paan-stained teeth that he had left.

'You're looking well,' Vinod said.

'Everyone that I grew up with is dead, including your father. But I am still here,' the old man sighed. 'It must be God's will. Come. Come.'

The old man held onto Vinod's arm with one hand and his walking stick with the other. They walked to the back of the Vinod's house and looked at the land stretching out for some distance.

'See all the land up to the highway on this side?' the old man said as he gestured with his stick.

Vinod nodded. The highway lined by trees curved its way in one direction to Navsari and in the opposite direction all the way to Mumbai. There were colonies of houses all along the road.

'All this land is farmed and produces crops regularly. The government makes it's difficult for constructors to buy agricultural land but your land, which has not been farmed for years, is easier for them to buy.'

'Do you think I should sell up? This house and the land has been in my family for generations.'

The old man looked thoughtful.

'India is changing quickly Vinod. None of my grandchildren will want to work on the land. They will get good jobs in Mumbai or Bangalore or maybe they'll leave India. Like you did. My son will have to think about selling our land one day too, but not while I am alive. As Patels, this land is who we are, we are farmers, but times have changed.' He turned and smiled at Vinod.

'Listen to any offers. Ask them what they will do with your land. Remember that it will affect everyone in the village in some way. I have led the village panchayat for over thirty years and I can tell you that you will need the support of the village.'

'I won't make a decision without talking to you all first.'

The old man nodded.

'Look, over there.'

Vinod looked over and spotted some movement and flashes of iridescent blue in the foliage. He squinted his eyes and tried to identify what he was looking at, but he couldn't be sure.

'Peacocks!' the old man exclaimed. 'They're looking for food and at night they roost in your mango trees.'

'My God! I've never seen them around here before.'

'No, they appeared a few months ago. Two peacocks and nine females.'

They could hear the distinctive squawking of the males.

'They were noisy during monsoon when the males were trying to attract females in their harem. They walked around with their feathers fanned out. Such beautiful colours. Soon their eggs will hatch, and they will look after the chicks. Go take a closer look.'

Vinod walked closer to the birds. He could see the males, with their distinctive blue necks and their long trailing feathers. The females, huddled together in groups, lacked the trailing feathers and had bodies that were different shades of brown. As he got closer the males screamed louder and they darted towards the mango trees. One of the peacocks flew the short distance to the top of one of the trees squawking loudly in protest, followed by his harem of peahens. Vinod returned to his house where his neighbour waited.

'They love the mangoes off your trees. They also like some of the maize and corn from our fields too but we're not complaining. We like having them around and they will bring us luck. Lord Krishna will smile down at us,' the old man said.

'They're amazing,' Vinod said. 'I hope they stay. I'll bring Bhanu next time, I'm sure she'd love to see them.'

'They'll be here for a few months. They won't go anywhere until the chicks are hatched and they learn to fly.'

The sound of motorbikes interrupted them, and they made their way to the front. Two men sat on Royal Enfield Himalayan motorbikes in front of the house. Both had jeans, boots and T-shirts on and looked in their twenties. They were clean shaven with fashionable slicked back hair, short at the sides, and wore sunglasses. The old man made his way to his veranda and sat down gingerly on a chair. Both the young men stared at Vinod.

'Who are you?' Vinod asked.

'I'm Tej,' one of the men said.

'Muna,' the other one nodded.

Tej got off his motorbike and got a thick envelope from his shoulder bag. He handed it to Vinod.

'What's this?'

'Documents. Sign them,' the man said.

Vinod was taken aback. He pulled the documents out of the envelope. It looked like a photocopy of the deeds to his land and a sale agreement.

'I'm not signing anything,' he said emphatically. 'Who are you?'

'It's a good price,' the other young man said getting off his motorbike. He walked a few steps towards Vinod and undid his jacket. Vinod spotted a gun underneath and his heartbeat quickened. He looked at the documents again.

'Twenty lakhs,' he said.

The old man sitting on his veranda laughed.

'You know it's worth ten times that!' he said raising his voice.

'Stay out of this old man,' the young man warned.

'You are in my village! You don't tell me what to do,' the old man said raising his stick at him. 'You think because he is an NRI that you can cheat him? His father was a good friend of mine. We look after each other here.'

Some of the neighbours came out of their houses to see what the commotion was about.

'Who are you?' Vinod asked.

'Sign it yaar!' the young said raising his voice.

'I'm not signing this. Get out of here both of you before I call the police,' Vinod said.

'There's no Scotland Yard here to come running to help you,' Tej said with a laugh. The villagers gathered around them and stared at them defiantly. The young men weighed up the situation and got back on their bikes.

'You don't frighten me. Get lost!' Vinod shouted.

'We'll be seeing you. Maybe we'll drop by Kesar Society to see you and your wife,' Muna shouted. They turned their bikes around and roared off.

'Who the hell are they?' Vinod asked.

'I think they are Mohan Das's men,' one of the villagers said. 'I've seen them in Navsari.'

Vinod looked at his neighbour in amazement.

'This is India,' the old man said.

NISHA PATEL is a qualified accountant whose interest in writing started when she got pregnant. While on maternity leave, she started a blog about the trials and tribulations of parenting while trying to find a work-life balance. Over the years, Nisha realised how much she enjoyed writing and pursues it in her spare time.

Nisha writes stories partly in an attempt to make sense of this crazy world, and partly for the joy of writing. Her creative words have appeared in two anthologies, Tales from Garden Street and Small Good Things as well as online at The Drabble, 50 Word Stories and in the National Flash Fiction Day – Flash Flood. When not writing, Nisha is a mum and an accountant. She lives in Leicester with her husband and two young daughters.

When I was young, I would listen to lots of stories at dinner time about my grandparent's journey about coming to England, living and adapting to life in a new country and working hard to make a good life for themselves including overcoming all the obstacles and challenges they faced. 'The Fire at our Factory' is one such story loosely based on an event in my grandparent's life. I wrote this story from a female point of view living in England in 1966 where the internal struggles and resilience of women is often overlooked.

Nisha was mentored by Amanthi Harris.

The Fire at our Factory

Parvati followed the little flame as it hissed and flickered uncomfortably close to the brightly coloured picture of Lord Shiva in her little altar in the corner of her kitchen. In the picture, Lord Shiva is sitting in a meditative pose with his legs crossed in front of the Himalayas wearing a jagged sheepskin skirt. Parvati sellotaped this to the wall and placed a little brass murti of Lord Ganesh in front, slightly to the left. The flame kept blowing out this morning when Parvati tried to light the divo, a small piece of cotton wool dipped in ghee, and so she kept pushing it back. Eventually, almost reluctantly, it lit and stayed on.

Peeping at the flame to make sure it stayed safe, Parvati and her family sang the morning prayers as usual. Then they all bowed their heads and asked for their personal needs silently. Parvati whispers, 'Thank you God for giving me my beautiful family. Please God, let the factory do well. Let there be more orders and more work so that we don't have to struggle for money and food.'

Once everyone had finished, she got ready to cook for Dhiren's cousins who were coming over for lunch. Normally, she would have left the divo burning until it naturally ran out of ghee, especially with it being Sunday, but today she had chicken to marinate in spices and cook, coriander chutney to make and dhokla to prepare and so she took the bright pink rose that was in front of the divo and used it to put the flame out. Once it had cooled down, she threw the ashes in the bin with the match.

*

There was still life in the match that had been abandoned near the war shelter huts. The linger of the cigarette smoke wafted past while the unassuming arsonist quickly walked by. The glowing red head of the match started to feed off the small unnoticeable scraps of shredded newspaper that were lying around leading to the hut. The flame seemed to glow slowly at first, languishing in the dark wintry night, testing itself against the bitter cold. The newspaper had other ideas, curling up, turning black and gathering speed as it passed through several strips of newspaper and into the hut.

Two of these huts had been converted into a factory. In 1966, health and safety laws were not fully developed with regards to the storage and use of chemicals. The first hut was where all the manual work took place. The hand mixing of resin with varnish to fill the moulds, those in which the current transformers would be made. There were two large vats in the building, one full of resin and the other full of varnish. All primed and ready for Monday. All primed and ready and volatile.

The first hut was glowing orange before a loud explosion filled the air and sky. A few people driving past stopped to see what was going on. It was late in the evening and most people were at home. No one around here was working on a Sunday. And it wasn't a very busy road. But the orange glow could be seen for miles around and the fire engines were already on their way.

Dhiren's cousin had just left when the phone rang. It was unusual for anyone to ring after 9 pm and so instantly Parvati felt uneasy.

'Hello,' Dhiren answered cautiously. 'Oh! Hi Gulab, how are you?' Dhiren replied happily to his friend. Parvati smiled and went to clean up the kitchen. 'Amit was here just now, in fact, and we were just talking about how we haven't, all three of us, we've not got together for a while. What are you doing?'

Dhiren's tone changed. 'A fire? By the factory? Ok. Yes, yes, ok.' Parvati stopped what she was doing and waited for Dhiren to get off the phone.

'Come on Parvati. There's been a fire. No one's sure which factory but it might be ours. Let's go.'

Parvati got her coat and repeated Dhiren asked to make sure she had heard right, 'There's been a fire? By the factory? Let me sort the girls out.'

'Anila? Asha? I'll explain later but we're just going out. I'll let Mrs Smith from next door know we're going, and to keep an eye on you. Don't worry, we'll be back soon.'

'Mummy, mummy don't go.' Asha pleaded, 'When will you be back?' Anila asked. Both looked up to their mum with big scared eyes.

'We won't be long dhikri. I love you and you,' kissing them both on top of their heads. 'You have to be brave for your mummy and daddy now.' Parvati said trying to hide her panic.

Dhiren came in and said, 'Be good girls. Let's go, Parvati.'

After knocking on the neighbour's house and explaining the situation, they got into their Mini and drove down as fast as they could, to the factory.

Parvati twisted her sari into a tight rope as she sat in the car thinking about the fire. Why us? Was it something she had done? Was it because she had stubbed out the divo this morning too soon? Maybe Lord Shiva, the God of Destruction was unhappy with them and had come for their factory. She knew it was silly to think like that but she couldn't help it. She wanted to cry, to bawl her eyes out, to pull her hair and scream 'Why us?' but apart from being nervous about what they were going to see, she also knew that Dhiren hated any dramatic display of emotions. He was all for the British stiff upper lip.

They had worked so hard on this factory and to think it was all up in flames was more than Parvati could bear. She suppressed a sob as she thought about all the late nights they had slaved away - Dhiren working on his designs for the current transformers while she cleaned and painted and counted the actual transformers they were going to send to Hong Kong. They would stay up late talking about the transformers, about the customers, about the few people they employed. Dhiren quickly glanced at her but didn't say anything. She could tell he was worried too by the raised eyebrows and all the grooves on his forehead getting deeper ever since the phone call.

'What are we going to do?' Parvati asked trying not to cry. 'We've lost everything. Everything we've worked for is gone. What are we going to do?'

'Let's see if it is our factory.' Dhiren replied, 'Don't get upset yet. And if it is ours, then we will ask Gulab for some help or maybe I can go back to work at Sankeys again. Let's just see first though.'

She was still half hoping that it wasn't their factory but as they got closer, she knew in her heart that it was. Why else would they get called?

Dhiren gasped as they reached the factory. Parvati stared in horror at the fire in the first hut as the flame hissed and spat dangerously close to their Mini. Dhiren edged the car back before stopping. She could feel the heat and rage of the fire in the car and wanted to cry again. Not angry tears like earlier but from pure sadness of losing their factory and everything in there.

'Come on,' Dhiren said. 'We might still be able to save the paperwork.'

Parvati got out of the car remembering how only last month Dhiren had proudly told the girls how his transformers, his designs were being used to run the public trains in Hong Kong. He had recalled how a chance outing to the NEC exhibition eventually led to securing big contracts with two companies in Hong Kong. After years of struggle, they were getting to a stage where they could think about expanding, hiring more people, looking for a better place to work and now this.

The fire engines hadn't arrived so Dhiren said to Parvati, 'Let's get the designs and transformers out of the second hut before it's too late. Cover your mouth with the end of your sari and I'll use this hanky and let's get as much as we can out.'

'Are you sure we can do this?' Parvati asked getting her sari ready anyway.

'We have to try. Just follow me. They should all be in the cupboard at the back but there's some on my desk. You get the ones on my desk first and I'll start getting the ones from the cupboard. Come on.'

Some more people turned up to help but with it being chemicals, it wasn't easy. Parvati could feel everyone's eyes on her as she took a deep breath and followed Dhiren in. John, who worked next door joined them and between them they got a lot of their transformers and paperwork out.

Parvati had just picked up another transformer when she heard the wailing sirens of the fire engine get louder and louder and then abruptly stop. Parvati shuffled out of the way with a large transformer in her hand as the fireman instructed everyone to move further back. She watched the firemen take down the flames, feeling stunned and tired, barely able to straighten out her thoughts let alone say anything.

Dhiren said, 'I think we've got all the designs but I don't know what condition they are in.'

'I don't know when we will be able to go back in though. We did good though getting everything out.'

'Excuse me, yes, Hello,' Dhiren said to the closest fireman to him. 'When will we be allowed back in?'

'Not today Mr Patel. The fire's going to take a while to go down and then we won't know how stable the chemicals are. The earliest I would say is tomorrow morning. Probably makes sense to go back home now. Come back tomorrow.'

Dhiren nodded and turned to look at the fire deep in thought. Parvati stayed next to him watching everyone else follow the fireman's instructions and leave. Eventually, as the fire died down they left too.

At home, they emptied out the car and Dhiren started going through the paperwork.

'How are you? Was the fire at your factory?' Mrs Smith, the neighbour asked.

Parvati nodded and said 'Yes.'

'Oh, I'm so sorry.' she replied, touching Parvati's elbow. 'The girls were as good as gold. Haven't heard a peep from them all night.'

'Thank you.' Parvati replied as Mrs Smith let herself out.

Parvati went to check on the girls. Anila was fast asleep but Asha was still awake.

'Are you OK mum?' Asha asked, frightened at seeing her mum covered in black soot.

'Everything will be ok. I'll explain everything tomorrow but we're both home and both safe so go to sleep now.'

Parvati went into the bathroom to have a quick bucket bath to wash off the black soot. The water clattered loudly into the empty bucket disrupting her jumbled thoughts. What were they going to do now? How were they going to eat every day? How were they going to pay the bills for heat and light and water? As the bucket started to fill, the clattering stopped and the soothing gush of the water calmed her mind and she started to cry. All their years of hard work and they had nothing now. Their beautiful factory in ashes. Even though they had rescued most of the paperwork and some transformers, they had nowhere to work, no materials and no money. They were back to the beginning. In some ways slightly worse than the beginning as all their savings, excitement and hope had been extinguished with the fire too.

She went back into the sitting room where Dhiren was still checking the paperwork.

'You should go to sleep.' She said to Dhiren. 'Have a wash and go sleep. You... we can sort this out in the morning.'

'Yes. I just need to check a few more papers and then I'll do the rest tomorrow. Don't worry. I'll clean up in a bit, you go sleep.'

Parvati lingered for a little while, but her eyes were really heavy now and so she went to the bedroom. Dhiren would come when he was ready.

The next morning Parvati told the girls everything that had happened last night while she got them ready for school.

'There's been a fire at the factory.' She started, 'So we're going to have a lot of work at home until we can get something else. It was a big fire but no one was hurt. Everything is going to be ok.' As she finished plaiting Anila's hair. 'Let's do the divo and pray for lots of good luck for the factory. Lord Shiva destroys the old things to make way for the new things, so we'll be ok. Come on.'

Parvati gasped as the flame from the divo hissed and smoked dangerously close to Asha's school blouse as she walked past. She moved the divo slightly not wanting to snub it out today. Maybe she shouldn't have snubbed the divo out yesterday. The fire must have started small and tame, like this little flame. While this little flame was used to please the Gods, the Gods had not been happy yesterday. She needed their help today, some miracle or some way for them to keep working and providing for their girls.

Dhiren, however, seemed quite pleased, 'I think I've got all my designs. Of course, I'll have to write them out again but I have them all. And Gulab has offered us some space in his factory that we could use and do some work in.'

'I've got phone numbers for all our customers including our two biggest, Mr Chang and Mr Lei. I'll just explain to them, and all the others, about what happened. Everything should be okay. We'll be okay.' Dhiren confirmed happily.

Parvati took a deep breath. Her mind was racing all over the place. 'How are we going to reconstruct everything? We've put all our savings into this factory. We've sacrificed so much to get to where we are now,' she burst out. 'We've hardly got any money to get by on. What are we going to eat tonight and tomorrow and the day after? I've got a few potatoes for tonight so I can make potato curry but then what? What are we going to do?'

Dhiren looked surprised by the outburst, and didn't say anything. Parvati signed and got up to go to the kitchen. 'Look,' Dhiren said. 'I'll figure something out for the next week or so. But Gulab said we can work at his place so we can still get the orders out to Hong Kong and I'll call them and explain what happened and why we're a bit late and we have insurance which I'll call up tomorrow too. So we'll have some money coming in, we'll be ok. We just need to find a new place to work and we will be ok.'

He walked over to Parvati and gave her a hug. She nodded and then sobbed into his chest, something she had not done in a while, if ever. She knew it wasn't easy for him either but sometimes he was so obsessed with the factory, he didn't think of anyone else or anything else.

And she was tired.

So, so tired of scrimping and saving and working so hard. If only Dhiren had remained in his full-time job. He would have been a manager by now and they would all be getting along comfortably, just like Amit.

But, Dhiren had big dreams ever since he arrived in this country. She was in awe of him. His drive to do better and make something of himself was why she admired him so much and this was the life they had chosen. It was a small setback, she just needed to reframe her thoughts and get the strength from somewhere to match Dhiren's optimism and like she said to the children, 'Shiva is the God of Destruction, he only destroys things to make way for new and better creations.'

IONEY SMALLHORNE is a writer, poet and educator of Jamaican heritage from Nottingham. She's an alumni of Goldsmith College's MA in Creative Writing & Education, and an Inscribe Writer. Shortlisted for the Sky Arts/Royal Society of Literature Fiction Award 2021, winner of the Writing East Midlands/Serendipity Black Ink Writing Competition 2021, longlisted for Moniak Mhor's, Emerging Writer award 2024. Her short story, *First Flight*, appears in the first Black British speculative fiction anthology, Glimpse, 2022, (Peepal Tree Press), and her poems for children can be found in, *Spin*, 2024 (Otter-Barry). Ioney is a part time English teacher in FE.

After losing momentum with my writing schedule and failing to complete a short story, my mentor, Leone Ross, laid down a new law. For 14 consecutive days, she gave me an insanely tight word limit, a prompt, and a 24-hour deadline to deliver. 'Bloom' is one response to Leone's call to show up—an ode to trusting your ideas, riding out challenges, and finishing. Three cheers for Leone Ross! 'The Harp' was inspired by an image of the same title by Chris Van Allsburg.

Both stories explore the refusal to settle for prescribed conventions, the importance of honouring personal truths, and celebrating the off-centre.

Ioney was mentored by Leone Ross.

Bloom

When I was a girl, Mum told me never to let the breeze carry away the hair from my comb.

'A part of you will always be lost, wandering, looking for a place to root.' Mum warned.

I wondered if this was why the old lady down the street sang under the plum blossom. Had she let parts of herself go? The neighbours claimed Ms Kitty's stories were closer to cubic zirconia than diamond, but I thought she sang them and smiled with real commitment.

These days, arthritis has taken root in my Mum's joints. Her ankles, gnarled trunks. She looks out her window, sighing at the weeds.

When I was fired, from the good-good job in town, I decided to walk home, to pause and admire the rose-quartz plum blossom confetti the street. It had been years since Miss Kitty unfolded her chair and sung under it. She told me once, while I was skiving school, that she visited the tree around her birthday to remember how far she'd travelled, to remember the parts of herself that belonged here. She said she'd planted the tree at eighteen, before she left this city, to remind people to sweeten their days before winter.

Dandelions allow the breeze to carry their head of seeds, wherever it wishes, leaving their stalks bald. Look how their yellow spreads.

Before I left this city, I picked a handful of plums for the journey, bit into one, wiped the juice from my chin.

The Harp

The sulfureous rotten egg smell that deterred most people from walking the bogs didn't bother Mike. This marshland was a place of comfort—waterlogged, root-filled deep mud and peat, decomposing plant matter. And the spiny river trickled on by as it always did. The heavy eyelid of morning fog was yet to lift. The 5:53 train rattled the tired fences separating the terraces from the quagmire. It seemed to Mike that the train line, river, and footpath all curved in agreement round the back of houses, as if to say, 'nothing to see here, continue with your life.' It was there, where the river bent and spilled onto cattails and bulrushes, where the expanse of bogland blended with grey horizon, that the harp stood, like the skeleton of a giant wing trapped in mud.

Mike still wore his navy boiler suits, despite seven years retired. His lower back insisted the days of repairing gearboxes, fitting engines, and replacing exhausts were long-gone. But like any machine, Mike was made to work, to move, to do things. So each morning he'd wear his boiler suit and walk Branston, his attentive, beloved Staffy-Labrador mix, through the bogs. He experienced life like an engine: each cog and piston playing its part. He needed it to be like this. Ordered. As he crossed the bridge, the stench of hypoxia meant things were working as they should. The life cycle was turning. But there was a harp wedged in mud, amongst bulrushes and common reeds. He'd walked here only yesterday, and it hadn't been there, then. Why had it been disposed of here? By who? Hypnotised by this quandary, Mike blinked, squinted. Was it a harp? Could it be? Perhaps he was wrong. Was it a message from his mother?

Branston sensed his friend's stillness, stopped sniffing the ground, and made his way to Mike's side, using his wet nose to nudge the thinking man's hand, urging the morning walk on. Mike rubbed the dog's head and threw his favourite throw-fetch toy to steal a few more moments. Branston, fooled by the diversion, ran after the toy.

It was a harp, perfectly formed, wedged in mud and peat. A dropped pin to mark a destination. Mike was sure now. The sun broke through the clouds for a fleeting moment and the harp's nylon strings seemed to chime. He couldn't leave it. He came off the bridge and lowered himself into the bog.

Linda would have finished her first brew by now, would be packing a bag for her early morning swim; it was Tuesday after all. He could explain the mud by saying he got carried away playing throw-and-fetch with Branston, that the dog eventually refused to retrieve the toy but he couldn't leave without it – simple and believable, she knew he would do anything for Branston, the two of them inseparable. She would tell his son Aaron when he came over this evening for a rare visit, and they could tease him about it.

He paused, ankle deep, and looked at the harp again. What was he doing? This was ridiculous. He looked back to the spot on the bank where he'd first sighted the mystery, about two meters back, close enough to turn back and continue with the familiar walk; he could add the harp to all the other unanswered questions in his life. What had happened to his childhood pet cat, or his final science assessment he knew he'd left on Mr. Clarkson's desk. Why he was sacked from his first job when he was the best mechanic in the garage. No, he wanted this quandary answered, if there were no answers for other things. He wanted to pursue a mystery - just once. To feel the curve of the harp's face, to feel hard and real answers, to hold something he needed. The chance to be close to his mother, just once.

He surged forward, squelching his way through wetland, his steps slowed by the suction of mud. His body was heavy. His spine hurt. Why had he been an absent father to Aaron?

He was aware of Branston, returned triumphant with the toy, his victory faded to whining when he saw Mike knee-deep in the sludgy carbon sink. The dog tilted his head, pricked his ears, and whined again, refusing to support his friend's decision. They were usually heading towards the wooded area by now, the fetch-throw toy would have been lost and found a few times, but the 6:18 train was heading into the city, and the harp was reeling Mike in. He looked back at his loyal, handsome friend.

'You know about retrieving, boy, don't you?'

Branston's nose twitched as Mike turned in pursuit of the harp, sat fidgeting his bottom into the damp earth.

Why had his adoptive parents chosen him, thought Mike. And why had they changed his name? He had pondered these things before, of course he had, and many times, as a lad. But not for a long time now.

The harp was perched beyond a bog the size of a mini lake, and its floating islands of tall grasses acted like stepping stones. Mike moved more determinedly; climbed over tree roots, rocks, a small mound of fly-tipped trash; a rusty pram wheel, an oval rug, a rattan tray, sodden towels, beer cans, and crisp wrappers.

He needed to pluck a string.

Thigh deep in the stagnant brown waters, his feet like plunges on the swampy sediment bed, he grimaced as he lifted them. A rodent scurried to the edge. The harp stood on higher ground, water lapping at her ankles, like how the Bramble Bay coast had washed over Mary's feet when seven-year-old Mike nearly drowned.

'The boy should've learned to swim by now,' Roger had declared, dragging his gasping body from the water's reach. Mike's favourite toy car had slipped from his hand into the sea's silvery cold clasp and he'd gone to save it. 'If you want something you'd better work for it,' Roger had said, refusing to retrieve it. 'Tears won't get you anywhere.' He remembered the rage filling his small frame, how he'd launched his whole body after his toy, the salt burning his eyes, how he'd panicked in the all-encompassing cold. He was smaller than average, a legacy of malnutrition, a legacy from his life with his birth mother, Alphia, they said. But Roger and Mary had been sent by God, and he ate three meals a day and went to Mass and a proper school with white children, and his adoptive parents had made him a well-rounded boy who should be able to swim. 'The water didn't even come to his navel!' He remembers Roger's disgust at his coughing and gasping, how a small circle of beachgoers had crowded into the early summer Sunday. The beachgoers had been perplexed by the Black boy with white parents even before the drowning episode. Mike's body had always created a scene: an uncategorised sea creature hauled from the depths into unfamiliar daylight; was it a mammal or amphibian?

Mary stood with a towel, waiting for Mike to get to his feet.

Each step forward was laboured now, but the harp was an instinctual call, inaudible to anyone else, a whispered invitation. A magpie landed on the harp's neck and pecked at the tuning pins, its raspy cackle mocking Mike's predicament. He swung his arms through the air, hoping the momentum would carry his lower body through the weight of water.

After the beach scene, Mike learned it was better to submerge his feelings, to keep them under the surface along with the memories of Alphia. His life presented many opportunities to practise this skill: meeting his Roger's and Mary's relatives at family occasions, 'Oh, he speaks so clearly. If you heard him speak without seeing him you'd never guess, would you?' At Parents' Evenings, Roger and Mary always received the praise as if they'd done something, despite how hard Mike had studied. 'It goes without saying that the progress he's making is due to your patience. God will bless you,' said his teachers. Mike pushed his feelings away when the boys held him down longer than necessary in the rugby scrub, when the lady across the road rubbed his head for luck before going to the races. All of this, swallowed down, along with his questions.

Mike trips on something beneath the water: his hands instinctively reach out, trying to protect his face from the sludgy deep mess, but his body is briefly submerged. The soft mud dampened the cracking sound of his left ankle but he feels it, he feels everything. As he lifts his upper body from the brown stagnant water, his cries disturb three wood pigeons on a branch; they flutter and fly to safety. Back in safety, Branston barks, jumps back and forth between firm land and swamp as if contemplating rescue.

He was nine when he successfully swam to the other side of the pool, gaining his 25-metre badge and certificate, but his mother kept it from him, saying he would only get it dirty, she'd keep it with his other records. He remembers how his father went to a convention alone because his mother had sprained her knee, how he crept downstairs when she was asleep, opened the drawer in his father's study to look for that swimming certificate but found lots of papers with his name typed on them instead. Teacher reports, medical records, adoption papers. He remembers imagining how clouds must feel, storing all that water, waiting for a time to pour a deluge. How a simple sheet of paper could hold so many secrets about a real mother; Alphia Moore, musician…harpist…sectioned…unfit.

Mike remembers when he was nineteen and his father died of a heart attack, how it felt like the shock of cold water from Bramble Bay, but this time he could breathe, deep and clear.

Mike's relatives talked to Mary, saying inheritance was for bloodlines. All he asked was for the folder about Alphia, for it to be taken out of the dark drawer, into the light, but his mother said his father burned it before he died.

The harp stood like a headstone. Mike, salty-eyed and exhausted, considered the instrument, still around ten meters out of reach.

He clung onto a dead tree trunk, caught his breath, his pain pulsating but he felt a clarity that he hadn't felt before. Pain can do that, cut through the blur and comfort of lies. He grappled with his wet weight and with the thought of not reaching the harp. Anger brewed like bile.

He thought of the draw that was kept closed for all those years and pushed himself forward. He thought of all the MOT's and gear boxes he'd fixed, cars that he'd bought back to life with the right part. He heard Branston paddling towards him.

'Come on boy!' Encouraging his loyal friend and himself to keep moving. And they both did. Mike let go of holding things in. He released a guttural shout from his childhood. The trees and cold water held it gently. It was time to release his cloud. He grunted and cursed with each lunge forward. He imagined his lungs like pistons, each inhale deep, each exhale a pained growl. The swamp rising to his waist. Branston who wasn't slowed down by the suction of mud swam ahead and reached the mound where the harp stood first. Mike threw his body forward and landed at the base of the instrument, wheezing.

Later, in hospital, they will say the Harp didn't exist. But it did for Mike. He plucked a string and remembered his mother's voice.

MICHELLE WALES Throughout thirty years of teaching, I have incorporated the arts wherever possible. Increasingly, I have become disillusioned with the neoliberal policies and marketization of education. In 2023 these gave me the impetus to seek creative and holistic ways of working. I trained with the Birmingham Rep Theatre's Foundry programme in workshop facilitation. I spent three months at SAMPAD, a South Asian art company based at the MAC, as a trainee creative producer and have returned to work with them on numerous occasions. In 2024, I worked for the Birmingham Hippodrome as an associate producer and trained with Create Central and the Red Earth Collective. I am a third-year doctoral student at Birmingham City University. My work looks at children's literature through the lens of Critical Race Theory using arts-based methodologies.

Michelle was mentored by Leila Rasheed.

Jonathan Strong

JONATHAN – November 1764

Jonathan tentatively touched the bump on his temple, which was getting larger by the minute.

He licked the salty tears springing unchecked from the corners of his eyes, with his tongue.

His lip was gashed and sore. As he ran his tongue across his teeth, he could feel that his tooth had been chipped.

The force of the handle, of the small but lethal pistol, with which he had been beaten over and over, had left him with welts and bruises.

He winced as each tiny movement sent shooting pains across his aching shoulders, the core of his spine, and the back of his knees.

It was that blow to the back of his knees that had made him buckle, fall forward like a great felled tree, crashing at an unstoppable speed, sailing over the five or six wooden steps, and landing with a thud on the cold stone floor of the cellar.

Nearly six foot tall but only but only seventeen and some months, his height often got him in trouble, people supposed him to be a man and found a boy instead.

Laid a yoke on him that was too heavy.

Unguarded, he was unable to soften the fall with his hands.

The fall had caused the bump that was rapidly increasing in size, the cut lip, and the chipped tooth.

The fall had caused tears, mucus, and blood to mingle and merge, to create little unchecked rivulets.

Made him feel conscious, aware of just how alone he was.

The Demon had caught him unawares,
the pinched-faced white man, with his soulless grey eyes
and his Godless demeanour.

Demon, otherwise known as David Lisle, esquire.

On that first day in February 1764, when he first clapped eyes on Rotherhithe and then on David Lisle esquire, Jonathan had a faint hope that things might not be so bad, if he worked hard and did his best to please his new owner.

Lisle had stood at the edge of the dock, rubbing his thin-skinned, blue-veined fingers, and at first, he had seemed comical to Jonathan, who had never seen such outlandish clothing.

He had noticed his white wig, perched precariously atop his head; an oversized black cape, which served to highlight his pallid skin; and his unfashionably elaborate cravat; its cobalt blue contrasting against the ominous dark grey clouds. His dog strained on his tethers.

The chill of that February morning had dampened Jonathan's threadbare shirt and had heightened the discomfort of his makeshift footwear, but nothing had chilled him as much as that first look of contempt, that the Demon had thrown his way.

'Maybe,' thought Jonathan, 'maybe, if I had'na looked pon de Demah, straight in him eye, him might'a left we alone.'

Demon had BOUGHT him from the ship's captain.

A business transaction, like he was a sack of cassava or a bale of cotton.

'Demah' was what his Granna, back on the island, called all white people.

Cold-blooded reptiles, brutal abusers, who had ripped him from his grandmother's warm embrace as she had pleaded, cried, begged, cajoled, and then finally screamed herself quiet.

Taking him, from her, was like prising a suck rock from its stony fortress.

A primaeval, guttural, unsettling, cresting and crescendo-ing birth scream had chilled the air.

He could still hear her screams as the cart in which he had been trussed up rolled further and further away from the fields where he had first played and then worked.

Later, in the ship, as he lay peering into the darkness, exhausted with grief, paralysed with fear, he could hear Granna's screams, replaying them over and over in his mind, as lucid as if it were the here and now.

Iron cartwheels turning, turning, turning, throwing up dancing dust particles.

He watched them helplessly from the floor of the cart as they settled in ones and twos, uninvited, on his sweaty body.

The pound, pound, pounding of his heart evoking the pound, pound, pounding of the women beating the cassava at sunset.

Grinding it down, sifting through it, removing errant pieces.

Pounding and grinding, sifting, and cleaning, pounding, and grinding, sifting, and cleaning, trying to make the cassava more palatable for the children.

Cassava bread, baking on an open fire; lighting up the darkness of the night, and the darkness of their lives; sweetening it with sucre, siphoned into rustic vessels, fashioned from cane, sewn into the hidden folds of their cotton skirts.

Sweetening the night with pilfered sugar, unchecked laughter, song, lamentations, and love.

These were the lengths these sister-women had to go to, to bring some sweetness into their salty lives. To add some contrast to their stifled existence.

Pounding and grinding, sifting, and cleaning, pounding, and grinding, sifting, and cleaning; trying to make it more palatable for the children.

To feed the men hope and to nourish the children's souls.

Children like him.

Children of the enslaved, working in the blistering sun, with their sun-kissed, emaciated bodies.

… Panic.

A rough piece of cotton is shoved unceremoniously into his mouth and tied with sacking to muffle his cries.

Panic.

He is manhandled, hoisted up by the two men, and thrown unceremoniously across the hard cart: like cargo hitting decking.

Thwack!

Panic.

A fortuitous placement of stacked hessian cushions his fall. He hurts wherever his body has made contact with the unyielding cart.

Panic.

His silent screams reverberate in his head.

Panic.

His throat is constricted.

Panic.

In this way, bound and gagged without knowing why, the minutes merge into hours as his two captors jabber on noisily, unruffled, unperturbed.

Consciences clear.

He weeps.

He remembers.

He evokes.

The lullaby of Granna…

the singing and the humming…

or is it a buzzing in his head…

or the buzzing of mosquitoes…

unbridled access to his sweet 'n' salty skin…

feasting…

feasting…

carrion, but he is not dead,

is he?

Merging with the turning wheel, the singing and the humming, or is it a buzzing in his head, eyes betray him, or do they try to protect him?

Closing him into the deafness of sleep; sounds like thunder forming, or raindrops falling,

or trouble looming, or trouble looming, or trouble looming, these abductors, put an ever-increasing distance, between him and Granna.

So, now he knows for certain, that he will never be able…

to retrace this path,

to look for the right star,

to find his way back to the safety of that embrace.

She, who holds him tightly, in his dreams,

whispers soothingly,

hushes his panic,

helps regulate his breath,

strokes his curls,

touches his cheek with gossamer kisses,

so that all her love can flow to him,

and she pounds cassava, and she dreams of SLAUGHTER,

And ALL he has known thus far is ENDING for this boy.

Jonathan's eyelids finally flutter, close heavily, shutting out the light and the darkness, shutting out his pain and fear.

And, for a long while, he is rocked asleep by the soothing rhythm of the cart swaying, making its way

across the dusty hills, further and further from Granna and the fields of his boyhood, to the port,

where he will be transferred to the pit of a pitching vessel across an unforgiving ocean.

He can't pronounce 'Grandma' anymore since the blow to his mouth knocked some of the letters out.

Knocked out the control he had over his lips.

When he dared to call the man who was his papa, the man who sired him, 'papa.'

That heartless Shackler. Rapist.

Knocked out his ability to call out the name of the one person he was certain loved him in this loveless existence.

Falling in and out of consciousness now, in this place, in this dark cellar in London where he has been imprisoned, dreams of her crash in.

GRANDMA

Her screaming rage has dissipated and turned into a mournful whimper.

She knows that he is taken and won't be back. Her Jonathan.

She peers into the assembled faces of the dark-eyed sister-women.

The sister-women who had pinned her back then as they do now, fearful of what might happen if she confronts Massah again.

They hold and comfort her.

They rub balm on the scars of her coarsened hands and lanolin into her aching skull.

They bathe her feet in eucalyptus leaves and make her sorrel, pimento, and moringa tea.

They sing the soothing songs their mothers sang; with words they no longer understand.

And the darkness has returned to Granna's eyes, and the light has left her soul.

She closes her eyes but she can't un-remember.

More than sixteen years have passed but she remembers it as if it happened yesterday.

She hears the swish of the lash too late, and as she turns away from it, it catches her,

nearly taking out her eye.

Granna stumbles backwards.

He seizes the moment to grab her whimpering child and wrench her out of the cabin and into the woods.

Light and words have been taken away from her when she returns. Shame engulfs her.

Later the evidence of what has been done begins to show, with sickness and the roundness of her daughter's belly.

She re-sees those startled doe-eyes pleading for relief.

Smells his musky stench, wafting in through the window.

Guilt keeps him hovering nearby, that night, while her daughter screams.

Those fragile hips would not yield.

Granna remembers the softness of her molasses-coloured skin against her coarsened fingers.

Inhales the sweetness of her sweat.

Listens anxiously as she gasps for air.

She had lain next to her daughter through that night, waiting, waiting for her young body to yield.

The sister-women, singing, soothing, bathing and coaxing the girl.

And as she watches her daughter's life draining away, Granna becomes enraged.

She suddenly hurls herself across the small cabin with unexpected ferocity, crossing the tiny space with just a few easy strides, before the other women can react.

She knows where he is, lurking in the shadows, polluting the air.

She pounds him hard with hands strengthened by years of unrewarded toil.

'He has to go into the big house, by the back door, no better than a slave,' she rages.

'No better, but a whole lot worse.'

Her speed in the darkness catches not only the sister-women but him off guard.

She pummels him until the punch he deals her enfolds her in darkness.

When she awakes, it is to find herself in the arms of her sister-friends.

They have taken her daughter's body leaving behind the pool of ox blood red, soaked into the ground, which will not be washed away.

They pass her the bundle, the mulato child.

His skin, evidence of the-sin-of-the-father, but whose eyes are those of her daughters.

Brutality has been transmuted into the beautiful, caramel-eyed Jonathan.

Conceived without consent.

Harbinger of death.

His beginning, the ending for his fledgling mother.

Her daughter.

Bit by bit, this doe-eyed Yella baby laughs his way into her affections and takes hold of her heart with his little hand.

Against all expectations,

she loves him more than she should.

Granna names him after that obscene overseer who sired him.

Lest we forget.

But also names him 'Strong', in recognition of where he had come from, and how far he would have to go.

But the night that Jonathan is taken, handed over by the very same man who sired him the rage, the wrath, the vengeance of a wide-eyed Granna and Mama begins to stir.

Restrained by the sister-women, for now

The ancestors incessantly whisper…

Take up your cutlass, warrior woman, take up your cutlass and let his insides out.

Let the rivulets of blood which poured from your woman-child, also, spill from him.

The rivers of blood stain your wooden shack.

Rage.
UNLEASED.
Who created this child, BECAUSE, HE, COULD

Later that year, eight slaves, including Granna, are hung on the Frontier Estate, St. Mary's, Barbados. The same year, 1764, Jonathan was taken, never to return.

Granna smiles as the noose goes over her head because all that could be found of the overseer was his bloody 'kerchief', placed next to where they had laid her daughter's body.

Granna mixes drops of his bad blood with shavings of bone.

She evokes the spirits of the ancestors and pleads with them for help. Taking her last breath, and the bad blood that has been spilt, she and they forge a golden filigree ring with a blood-red ruby stone.

From evil, goodness is born.

At that very moment, as Granna takes her last breath,

Jonathan dozes fitfully, in and out of sleep on the cellar floor.

When next he opens his eyes, the talisman unbeknown to him has placed itself in his pocket, glowing gently and emitting light.

This is not the first time that this man, David Lisle esquire, has beaten Jonathan, however, it will be the last.

For, this beating is to change the course of history.

Jonathan Strong.

IMANI WENHAM is a writer and performer based in Leicester. They are the founder of Apittame arts, an organisation dedicated to showcasing stories from marginalised creatives and fostering community. With roots in Barbuda, Nigeria and Dominica, Imani brings a diverse perspective to their work. They have been part of various programmes such as Five O Fresh with Theatre 503, the Old Vic Theatre Makers, and National Theatre's Young Writers Programme. She has performed as part of There's no Racism in the UK by Lyla's Place and on a podcast with Thrive Theatre.

'Beaches Barbies and Bakeries' tells the story of Ines' journey from the Caribbean to England, capturing her search for belonging in a foreign land. Inspired by my Caribbean ancestry, this deeply personal story was first conceived when my grandmother and her siblings shared their first impressions of England. My grandmother told me she thought white ladies looked like walking dolls and that houses were ovens because of the clouds of smoke pumping out. This image stayed with me, shaping the heart of this story. While 'Beaches Barbies and Bakeries' is a work of fiction, pieces of me are threaded throughout—memories passed down, cultural echoes, and the emotional weight of migration. Through Ines, I explore the complexities of leaving home, the realities of arrival, and the enduring pull of the past.

Imani was mentored by Ashley Hickson-Lovence.

Beaches, Barbies and Bakeries

There were five of us. Me arriving last. Everything was irie when we was back home: no troubles, just the sun, the sea and me. I could go where I pleased without Mummy and Daddy worrying.
Nowhere to hide.
Nowhere to get lost.
Just me and my island full of love.

The sun beamed fire-hot, every day on my skin. Running down, the street barefoot. The red sandy roads would cake my feet.

My biggest problem was whether Adie had picked fresh genips for us to eat on our way to school. Adie would grin and pass a handful to me, 'Yuh lucky i nearly nam dem all.' Tearing through the hard green skin and devouring the tangy sweet yellow flesh of the fruit.

Sounds of the sea crashing against the shore, Daddy in his fisherman boat waving to us, while me, Ernest, Elijah, Hilroy and Adie danced on the beach. Laughing while we made our way home, the smell of Aunta Hilda cooking us dumplings and saltfish greeting us at the door. Out of breath from running up down, we made ourselves a brebrich; brown sugar, a hint of lime and cool water mixed together. Sipping it down while we watched the sunset from our window.

In the mornings, like her shadow, I would follow Mummy. To the brick house bakery, smoke pumping out the top. I would always sneak a bite, of the soft, sweet and warm bread. Spending sunrises and sundowns in my pocket of paradise.

I remember when that all changed.
I was ten.
Daddy came home, still smelling of his work.
The fish in the sea clung to his dungarees.
Slamming a poster on our table.
We had been called to England.

Big And Bold: Join In The Efforts To Help Build Back The Empire.

Mummy kissed her teeth 'Wah dem want wid us? We nah gih dem enough'.

Mummy stood, over the stove
simmering: bubbling and brewing.
She mixed the soup hard.
Stirring quicker and quicker.
The juices spilling out.
She turned to Daddy
Just staring at him.
Daddy brushed off Mummy's bad mind and said 'Tink of da pickney dem.'

So it was done, Daddy chose.
We were leaving our home behind and going to a foreign land.

Mummy and Daddy went first, to find where we could call home – then called for Hilroy and Adie.

Leaving us three behind.
Ernest, Elijah and I.

I spent my days in the sun, wondering if I was guilty of a crime.
Why did they leave us behind?
My pillow never dry.

On this island, the moments I had with them started to fade in my mind.

*

I was called at fifteen.

Five years of blonde dollies being sent to me.

Five years of empty words on white sheets.

Five years, would they even recognise me?

So again Daddy, had chose.

No warnings, no talking, no asking.
Just telling.
It was time for us to leave.

I thought one day I would be back.
Back here, back home.
I didn't know, we were leaving everything.
The sun, the sea, the joy.
Everything that did not fit in our suitcases.
We was up before the sun.

Aunt Hilda got us dressed, Sunday best.
Ernest and Elijah in matching tan suits.
Her yellow dress, she gave to me.
She said it was to borrow, but it ended up being something to keep.
She said 'Mi wan yuh fi look yuh best.
Nuh look suh sad Ines.
You will soon.
Be back wid mi.'
She squeezed us tight.
I tried to take a snapshot of her light.

We three sat at our terminal.
Ready to depart.

This small island will always have a piece of my heart.

I thought on the plane about, Aunt Hilda cooking us cornmeal for breakfast, hearing her laughter echo in my mind.

When we stepped off the plane, the ground was concealed by a blanket of powdered sugar. The cold air bit at me, and my eyes began to water. No amount of licking my lips was gonna get rid of this dryness.

Daddy and Mummy looked so different, their brown skin once warm, now faded- dulled by cold and time. If not for his thick curly hair and broad nose, Daddy could almost pass as a white man.
I had wanted this moment, dreamt of this moment.
They Shook my hand pulling me into their world.
As if I was a worker, not blood they had created.
No warm hugs, no soft words.
Just hunched backs, tight firm hands- carved with cracks from hard work.
I followed them in silence to the car.

Brick houses with smoke pumping out the top, row after row on the drive to our new home. 'Why is there so many ovens Daddy?' looking at me in the car mirror Daddy said, 'Dem is houses.'
We drove on in silence. Looking out the window, paved grey streets, houses that all looked the same.
Back home you could feel the heartbeat of the street miles away.

The houses painted bright colours.
Our home, in my pocket of paradise.
Was yellow.
With Pink- framed windows.
Mummy had sweetened Daddy for time for those windows.

Laughter, the steel pan players practising and the sweet smells of Hilda's world-class Sunday dinners floated through my mind.

As we pulled up to our new home, there was Adie and Hilroy, scrubbing red paint off the door. Big and bright words splattered

Go Home MONKEY!

I could feel them watching.
I felt like an animal, being prodded and poked.
All the white faces murmuring behind netted curtains, eyes on us, waiting for us to crack,
waiting for us to go running back,
dem beg us,
to come build,
back dey dutty cuntry,
dem lie,
streets paved with gold,
dat is what we was told,
in fact it is…

a golden stream of piss.

What kinda cuntry is dis?

Mummy quickly pushed us all into the house. Daddy not far behind dragging our bags inside.

The house was silent, we just stood.
In the hallway.
Not saying a word, we watched one another.

The walls were bare, the wood floor unfinished and one single picture was pinned to the wall.

A picture of us back home, smiling.
In our Sunday best.
Yellow house.
With pink window frames to match.
All together.
My family, thats the family I know.
Not these strangers in front of me.

Adie showed me to our new room.
Walls painted a faded yellow.
With two beds. Each with, a thin blanket and Chester drawers by the side.
Adie pointed to the bed on the left.
As I sat down, I felt the springs digging into me.

Adie without a word, began to unpack my bags.
Stuffing clothes into the draws.
Her face was screw up.
I tried to make Adie laugh by dancing.
Adie used to love to dance, in the sun, we would sway in time.
A leap, a jump, whatever steps Adie came up with to keep us all smiling.

If I could make her laugh, maybe she would come back to me.

'Wah wrong wid yuh?' I said to Adie.
She must have forgotten,
She needs to remember.

I need my Adie back.
Who held my hand tight when walking the red sandy road.
Who taught me how to swim.
Who taught me to dance.
I need my Adie who had taught me everything.

I went to grab her hand.
She looked at me, finally.
In the corners of her mouth, a smile was forming.
Until we heard the creaking steps, snatching my Adie from me.

She pulled away and grabbed my shoulders.

'Stop it now or Daddy–' The slow, heavy thuds of his boots cut through our moment. We froze.
She turned from me and went back to unpacking,
I was left standing alone, in the middle of the room.

'Come eat,' Daddy stood outside. The first dinner. The air was thick, the layers of things left unsaid. Hilroy jumped up, ran upstairs and came crashing down with a box of dominoes. We started playing, nothing was discussed that night or any night, but I felt the words flutter through the room, even though they never left the tips of our tongues.

*

The next day at school, followed by cold blue eyes, words like daggers danced around my ears.
My uniform was stiff and itchy, the cold creeping through the cloth to pinch at my skin, my fingers, numb.
Pale faces, blurring together, they looked like perfect dollies in the shop windows.
I was an ink stain, on the page of white.
I could hear laughter, shoes scraping on the ground, and voices rising in play.
A shadow hung over me, I was alone.
Then, like the sunrise.

I saw her across the playground.

A brown girl, just like me. She had two thick, coiled puffs full of life on top of her head. As soon as she set eyes on me she smiled at me.

We just stared.
She broke the unspoken rules and like a magnet, she pulled herself to me.
Every step she took.
The eyes turned to see.

Like we was in a zoo.
Two rare black girls.
Coming together.
The whites.
Bemused.
What was wrong with her?
She paid them no mind.
Only looking at me.

I wanted to become the dirt.
My heart was pumping, all these eyes on me.
She no had no intentions of making herself small.
Every move she made, was meant to take up space

Her skin was smooth, shining from Vaseline.

'My name be Judy,' she winked and leaned in close.

Her voice, like a paradise breeze, wrapped around my ear drums.
She struck me- high cheeks, brown eyes full of life and a smile that took over her whole face.
She stood before me as my first friend.

Judy said to me. 'Yuh dun forgot how fi speak?'
'I-I am Ines'
Before I could say more the bell rang. Teachers pushing us into line, Judith disappeared into the sea of white.

All day she ran through my mind, I spent the day thinking, is she real?

At the end of the day, she was standing at the gate.
I said 'You waiting for anyone?'
Judy said with a laugh 'Yeah…you.'
She locked my arm with hers and we walked.

The winter air was biting at my fingers but I felt the sun was right by my side.

For the first time in dis dutty cuntry, I didn't feel small. Judy pulled me into her world. It was no longer just grey, with Judy I finally started to see colour again. I started to find a reason to stay.

As soon as I stepped into the house, my whole body began to clench up. The cold returned. Their words clashed like pots and pans. Their bitterness for each other, beat throughout the house. Filled with poison, they ripped into one each other, hoping to get deep into each other's skin.

Their voices rising to be on top of one another. Wrapping me up in a suffocating quilt of chaos.
I crawled up the steps, every creak snapping the strings in me.
I did not want to be seen.

I closed my eyes and I saw her face. I felt her warm embrace, seeing Judy in my daydreams drowned them out

In the morning. The silence hung in the air but I did not miss the noise.
No one wanted to meet each other eyes. Mummy had made cornmeal, it was clumpy and bitter.
No cinnamon straws.
I took big mouthfuls, I wanted to get out of the house.

Judy was standing at the end of my street, with a lit white stick between her fingers. The smoke all around her, her afro was her halo in the sun. The colour of her hair, it was burnt orange when the light shined through it.
She caught me staring at her, she lifted up her hand for me to follow her up the street, her bag slipping off her shoulder. She started singing my name and making up some childish rhyme.

'Ines, ines
She really be da best
All di fine
Boi wan fi touch
Her-'
My face flushed hot with fear,
I fear Daddy could be somewhere near.
I grabbed her and put my hand over her mouth to stop any of the sounds coming out.
I pressed my mouth against her ear, 'Wah wrong wid yuh nuh.'
I could feel white eyes on me, crawling all over my skin.
She bit me and whispered into my hand 'Nuh worry bout dem ras.'

Her cheeks lifted into a smile.
The longer she looked at me the faster I could feel my heart racing.
I don't know what it was, but something was growing in me for her. 'Mi hava surprise, yuh guh love it.' As we walked she told me about her cousin. He was having a blues party. She squeezed my hand and ordered me to come to her house after school.

*

After school Judy took me to her house, she was an only child. Her room was painted a bright yellow, posters were pinned all over the walls. Her floor was soft. In the corner was a drum.

A shelf full of books. I sat on her bed, and the sheets hugged me like they already knew me.
'You hava come', Judy held a pink dress to her body, it was the same shade of pink as my pink framed windows. She spun around in the mirror. I tried not to stare but I could not help but take in her every move.

She took a seat on her bed next to me, leaning towards me.
I could smell her rose perfume and the coconut oil mixed with lavender in her hair. My ears started ringing, my throat began to feel like it was closing up, I was holding my breath and waiting for her to make the next move.
She was so close, I could feel her breath on my neck.
What was she doing?

I didn't care.
I wanted to be close to her.
Then we heard the sound of the front door being unlocked.

She jumped and went to open her bedside table. She pulled out her camera and placed the cold metal in my hand.
'Take a picture.'
She placed her hand over mine and showed me how to frame her.
She posed and directed me in what was the best lighting, to shoot her in.
I snapped the photos.

I hoped they would capture a piece of her essence on film, I could keep forever.

*

The full moon was out tonight, bright in the midnight sky.
We stood under the weeping willow tree, her hands locked into mine.
She in her pink dress, pressed up against me.
I stood staring into her.

I could feel her breath catching onto mine.
She kissed me, the taste of cherry liquor on her lips.
My feet planted into the ground.
Taking root into this moment with her.

Under the weeping willow, the world felt far away.
She pressed her forehead to mine, and for a moment, there was nothing else—just us, the full moon, and the breath we shared.
I wanted time to stop, to let this be forever.
But even as we pulled apart, I knew.

Whatever came next, she was a part of me now.

DIONNE WHITTER is a writer-director hailing from East Birmingham, with a focus on crafting immersive science fantasy worlds. A University of Westminster alumna, she draws inspiration from biofuturism tales that challenge how we perceive our place in the natural world. She is also a fan of classic movies like *Nausicaä of the Valley of the Wind*. Through the Middleway Mentoring Programme, she has learnt to embrace a mindful approach to storytelling, exploring the balance between nature and technology – past and future, faith and knowledge. As an aspiring author, she invites you to journey into the realms crafted upon the page.

In an alternate realm where technological wonders exist alongside lost knowledge, Hiroshi, a brooding mercenary, becomes entwined with Princess Dreyana, a perceptive royal questioning her path. After discovering the lost half of her Angel Stone, he is thrust into the role of her royal guard, tasked with safeguarding her until a coronation that could unite Earth and the newly liberated Neptunian colonies. As they journey through the lush Sakuran Empire and across the arid Red Sand Desert, the pair unravel a sinister religious conspiracy that threatens their world. Together, they must confront hidden truths about faith, duty, and identity, forever altering their destinies and perceptions of life, death, and the cycles that bind them.

Dionne was mentored by Michael Donkor.

Towards Utopia

HIROSHI

Hiro opened his eyes suddenly aware he was in a younger body of his own. 'A trail of smoke is the first sign,' he muttered the words to himself over and over. He reached up to a nearby tree and hoisted himself up to the highest branch. With the newfound view, he could see the soul stone mines and roaming tribes of fox riders along vistas of red grass. Hiroshi looked out over them, snuggling into a spot at the base of a tree branch.

Around him, groups of armed men lay asleep outside their tents. Slit brows, unkempt hair, and bulging muscles— these defined the mercenary band he served. He had seen fifteen name days, and on his fourteenth, he decided he wanted to leave home. Where to, he hadn't planned, but ultimately his future had called out to him. It was a luring presence that had led the boy here, deep into the Red Desert, a province away— a military aid for the 21st band of Osterhagen militia for hire. On this night, he was tasked with being lookout. All was peaceful; it had been for the past two weeks of their campaign, but his group was still vigilant for the next sneak attack on the nearby soul stone mines.

The fox rider tribe had moved to the continent from the south centuries ago. While the Sakurans of his city dwelled within the confined walls of society, the fox rider tribes of Old Oshun traversed the land. Many were born within its salt. By the time they grew into adults, they not only understood the spirit of land as they did their foxes but thrived alongside it. Despite the sandstorms, their ethos was to keep moving now that Old Oshun was in ruins. Fox riders had dark skin and full lips; he recalled the time his mother mentioned their hair, as soft as lamb's wool bleached golden by the sun. There was an exotic nature to their look, while native Sakuran features consisted of narrow, slanted eyes, rounded visages, and considerably lighter skin. Being a mercenary was the closest he would come to exploring their world.

'Bet they don't care about soul stones or owning land,' he sighed. The sky planet spun, containing rods of their own that he'd never see. Toward the ground, the last flames of the campfire had dispersed. Cups of ale lay dormant—some spilled into the soil. The petty Shogun who had funded the band's excursion cared. He had paid a great deal to show his care. Hiroshi guessed any man would do so to retain power. The moonlight poured into scattered rays that filtered through the canopy of the hideout. By now, the last of the fox rider caravan had moved on—the final protectors of the pack melting into the dark horizon. With them, Hiroshi's conscious state drifted away, guiding him into the world of sweet dreams.

#

The moon's rays of light had been overshadowed by sunlight, just as the night's silence had been overshadowed by the gray morning birds. Two things stood out against the usual early day: the absence of any smell and the silence where the clinking of armour should have been. Aside from the early morning dew, the aroma of cooked bird—typically the bandits' breakfast—had not risen to fill the air as usual. There was no sounds of clinking metal from his bandmates' armour. There was something, however: a faint retching in his ear. Hiroshi made his way down, careful not to fall from his position. There it was again—a coughing sound followed. Not a fox, but a man.

Hiroshi descended from the tree, his body unable to move fast enough. Still half asleep and gasping for air, he felt a fighting heart deep within his chest urging him to hasten. The last branch snapped beneath his feet, jerking his body forward. He fell flat to the ground, hit with a searing sprain in his ankle and a new smell. It had become familiar over his time supporting the mercenary band in conquering the soul stone mines of the Perth district of the Old Oshun Desert: blood.

He struggled to his feet and wiped the congealed sand from his face and arms. It was wet, with a grainy texture. More wailing filled the air. He looked up to see palpitating sheaths of flesh. Hiroshi followed the trail through the trees. Thick boot prints trampled the underbrush, leading back to the remnants of the campsite—or what was left of it. Tents lay stripped and collapsed on the ground. Beside them lay the lifeless bodies of his bandmates, their spirits now with the gods, leaving only their broken forms behind. By now, the ground had begun to soak with their decay. Others had been cut apart, some mismatched with limbs. Hiroshi couldn't help but gag. There was no holding back the bile from his stomach. To the ground he fell again, overwhelmed. He crawled toward the sound of an injured bandmate, uncovering the tarp from his body. Now he knew whose intestine he might have seen earlier.

'Are you okay?' Hiroshi asked, his voice trembling with fear.

'What does it look like, kid?' the man snapped.

'What should I do? I don't know what to do!' Hiroshi knelt next to the man, a spittle of red leaking from his mouth.

'Well, you could've stayed awake,' the man gasped, nodding toward Hiroshi and his sword nearby.

'You want me to?' His voice wavered, thick with revulsion and fear. The weight of the sword felt foreign, as if it were a cruel joke played by fate. It felt cold in his hand, heavier than he had expected. The man closed his eyes, and between laboured breaths, he said, 'It had to be your first time at some point. After this, you better run. Run, boy. Do you hear me?' Hiroshi looked at the sword, a tear in his eye.

'Did you hear me, boy? Don't be useless. Now do it. And run.'

A pause. His hands shook; the man had no choice but to lay there.

'Do it! Do I—' the man gritted his teeth, a final breath of release escaping him. With a trembling hand, Hiroshi plunged the sword into the man's skull. The sickening crunch of bone and the snap of spinal disks reverberated in his mind, a haunting echo he would never escape.

Hiroshi ran, wishing his feet could sprout wings. Not to his home, but to the unknown open lands. If fortune smiled upon him, he might stumble upon the next battalion. If he got his wish, however, he would run into the unknown and the secrets it held. The sun beat down on his back, and all that raced through his mind were the mercenaries' last few words: 'Did you hear me, boy? Do it! Run!'

The sword felt heavy in his grip, a chilling reminder of the choice he had made and the path he now walked.

#

'Did you hear me, boy?'

Hiroshi blinked. He found himself back at the Palace, in a small meeting chamber. He was standing in front of the Empress. Next to her stood a tall, dark-skinned man, staring at him. Three of the four royal Zenkai, who had tried to fight him, were lined up beside him.

'The Empress is speaking to you, boy.'

He looked at the tall man who had just spoken. Golden strands of his hair were braided back into lengthy, intertwined locks. The bright colour contrasted sharply with his rich skin but complemented his light-yellow eyes. The man stood with unmoving precision, still like a hawk. 'He looks like a fox rider,' Hiroshi thought, except he saw no fox at his heel. 'I wonder where his fox is, they usually never separate.'

'That will be enough, Amarr,' Biitna said, nodding her head to signal him to stand down.

'You will have to excuse the Great Zenkai. He takes his duties honourably, and I appreciate him for it. The time for pomp isn't now, however.' Hiroshi hesitated for a moment, but Biitna continued. 'The reason I summoned you is not to discuss your recent skirmish with my guards. I realize I haven't dealt with you properly since your entry into the palace.'

The royal Zenkai smirked at each other.

'You've been wandering my court, left to your own devices without receiving a proper reward for your hard work.' The guards' faces faltered – besides him they exchanged worried glances. Hiroshi stood back on the balls of his feet, unsure how to respond. 'In the old tongue, Zenkai meant to change for the better.'

Hiro looked around, expecting a hidden tone, but there wasn't one. The Empress continued. 'I see potential in you.' She sized him up. 'Do you see potential in you?' Hiroshi lowered his eyes from her imposing gaze.

'To tell you the truth, Your Majesty—'

'Excellency,' Amarr corrected him.

'Your Excellency. I'm not sure I believe in potential. You just exist as you are unless you become someone else. Imagining a fantasy of the future isn't real. Only now.'

Biitna raised a brow and turned to Amarr. She reached out a hand for his sword. Amarr complied, presenting his blade to her. Hiroshi could see the corner of her mouth curl into an intrigued smile. She turned back to him.

'Yes. You'll do well, Hiroshi,' she muttered to herself before addressing him with the sword resting on either side of his shoulders.

'Well, you were Hiroshi Sato; now you are Hiroshi Sato, Private Zenkai to Princess Dreyana Yil Neptune.' Hiroshi blinked in disbelief as the sword stood in Biitna's hands.

To his side, the three Zenkai opened their mouths in disbelief. Before an utterance of protest could escape their lips, Amarr whipped his head to face them. The glare in his eye communicated one thing and one thing only: 'Don't say a word.' That was all it took for them to get the message.

'Now go,' Biitna commanded firmly. Hiroshi, slack-jawed, turned to exit. Even moments later, he was still processing the previous interaction.

'While I deal with those who would dishonour my personal guest.' Now two venomous glares were directed at the guards.

Just as Hiroshi disappeared past the doorway, Biitna called out a final warning note.

'You'll find her downstairs. Protect her with your life, Zenkai.'

#

Hiroshi could see a blue light pulsating from the corner of the hallway. He was two floors down from Biitna's meeting rooms, now in the communal quarters, which housed the great hall, several banquet halls, and the Temple of Gaia. It was the oldest structure in the palace; in fact, the palace had been built around it. The porcelain tiles across the walls were now cracking at the edges but still maintained the gold-lined art indented in the centre. Regular windows were replaced with stained glass that depicted the goddess Gaia and her two brothers: Life and Death. From afar, the painting seemed like a nonsensical array of coloured glass tiles pieced together, but as he drew near, they blended into an illusory photomosaic. They seemed to be dancing in an endless circle. Hiroshi peered into the picture, noticing that the goddess was only holding hands with Death—a white-cloaked figure with a beaked mask and donning a farmer's scythe. The Harvester. In her other arm, she held a baby. Meanwhile, Life, also known as 'the tree from the seed,' was shorter and glowed a fierce yellow. He appeared to be scowling at his siblings, reaching out a hand with no rapport. Rays of light passed through the tinted glass in an intricate design that spiralled across the walls and flooring.

The temple's entrance was a narrow space and quiet, accommodating only a few at a time—usually for the morning and evening candle vigils. Hiroshi passed the stained windows, feeling the gaze of the immortalized historical figures follow him. He didn't dare to face them, knowing this was his first time entering a temple since he had left home. The shaming eyes of Mohammad the Blue Conqueror and especially the three eyes of Davas—a doll created by the god of Death himself—haunted his shadow. He looked forward to the light escaping under the temple doors.

He pulled the door open, and a blinding light emerged from inside. Hiroshi stumbled back, attempting to protect his vision with his forearm. Within the light, he could make out a figure who seemed to be floating on their back. Just above them was the beacon of light—small, yet capable of producing overpowering waves of radiance.

Hiroshi pushed forward through the flashes of light. Each step consumed his sight, burning the back of his retinas. He squinted and hissed at the stinging sensation. The source of the light doubled as the eye of the storm, increasing the airflow around him in a miniature hurricane. 'This can't be real,' he thought. Firmly, Hiroshi planted his feet, offering himself stability against the growing gusts of air.

'Hey!' He waved a hand in front of himself, trying to grab the figure but missed. 'Are you okay? Stay still; I'll try to get you out!' His voice was a small chirp that slipped into the howling winds. Still, the figure didn't stir at his call.

Hiroshi reached out again, this time managing to clasp the person's shoulders. 'Wake up!' He couldn't make out their face but proceeded to try and shake them awake. 'Come on!' His hands gripped deeper into the person's skin. 'Come on!' The last inflection in his voice boomed throughout the world, and the hairs on his arms stood upright against the skin—frosted by the nipping cold. He shook the person again; this time, their shoulder slipped through his grasp. The body hit the ground with a thud. At that exact moment, the source of light collapsed in on itself, and with it, the storm. Now the marble temple could be seen clearly. He was standing in front of a glass table with golden finishings displaying a large candle and incense shrine to the gods. Now, he could see clearly in front of him: the princess.

'Where am I? Take me back!' Hiroshi knelt beside the princess, her voice trembling with delirium. He used his hand to cradle her bruised head, although it was difficult because her flailing arms had almost hit his face several times. 'She needs me, I have to help her!'

She shook her head and attempted to get back up, but Hiroshi placed a hand on her shoulder.

'Help who?'

'I don't know, but she needs me. I have to go back.'

'Listen to me, princess—' His soothing words caused her to stop mid-thought.

She blinked a few times and tried to utter something more. He could feel a tremble run through her with each pause in her voice. The princess raised her hand to her forehead and closed her eyes for a brief moment.

'Wait, what is happening?' She sounded out of breath. Hiroshi looked at her furrowed brows, sensing her distress and confusion.

'My name is Hiroshi Sato. I saw a bright light and found you here.' He opened his mouth to tell her the rest of what he had seen; instead, he bit his tongue. That can come later. 'Are you feeling better now?' He noticed her darting eyes had settled to focus on him.

'Hiroshi.' she whispered.

'Those eyes,' he thought, 'like ice.' He cleared his throat to distract himself and then helped her up. 'Here,' he offered his hand. She took it.

The princess winced at the impact of her fall and took a moment to balance herself upright. 'I'll take you back to your room.'

The two walked a couple of paces back into the grand hallway, which connected the communal area to the residential quarters.

'So what was that back there? I've never seen anything like that in my life.' As he thought it over, the images of what happened in the temple etched into his mind. 'I know what I saw, and there's no way I hallucinated that,' he wondered to himself.

'I'm not sure,' the princess said, looking off to the side. 'This is the second time that it has happened, and I don't know why. It has something to do with this pendant.'

'I guess it's time you start to figure it out.'

They paused as the two turned a corner to the stairs leading to the residential quarters.

'Hiroshi,'

'Yes, princess?'

'The last time that happened, many of the court fell unconscious. Didn't you feel overwhelmed walking through the light?' He looked down at her and was met with a set of sparkling eyes. Hiroshi smiled but looked away to hide it— 'how long has it been since I've seen a friendly face?'

'I wouldn't be a good private Zenkai if I couldn't handle a bit of light now, would I?' He led her up a short flight of stairs back to her room. She turned to face him, her hand on the door handle.

'Who do you serve? I must be sure to put in a good word.'

'According to the Empress, you.'

The corners of the princess's mouth curled upward, not taking her eyes off him.

'Then you may call me Dreyana.' She turned the door handle to push herself in. A scent of warm almonds and lilies followed her. Dreyana turned back. 'And thank you, Hiroshi.' The door clicked shut.

He made his way down the velvet-lined hall, a lonely thought drifted across his mind: 'I don't know what happened in there, but something so powerful can't possibly be human.'

LYNSEY WILD Whilst growing up in the countryside, reading and writing were a lifeline for Lynsey's younger self. Having developed a passion for characters and stories, her writing currently explores belonging, identity and legacy. Lynsey has been working on a Women's Fiction book as part of Middle Way and also writes for children and young adults. Her academic background is in Media and Cultural Studies, and she previously worked in television. Lynsey is now a therapeutic counsellor with a special interest in adoption and identity. In her spare time, she enjoys live music, especially jazz, and appreciates animals and nature.

In this story, the space between being made to feel different and fitting in is explored. Nell internalises the racism she experiences and to compensate, tries really hard to impress. But something doesn't feel right.

Like Nell, I grew up in a place where I looked different to those around me and would often be made aware of it. Around eight years old, peer pressure can start to come into play, along with a growing awareness of self and others. Children can be exposed to things that might produce a whole host of negative emotions. So much so, it can feel too much to speak about. Whilst writing this story, I had in mind the importance of talking about these experiences and feelings to help avoid longer term damage.

Lynsey was mentored by Alison Woodhouse.

Nell Discovers: Not All Pain's the Same

At the beginning of her eighth summer, Nell stepped out of her house and ran straight to the bottom of her garden. Emerging from the shade of giant shrubs guarding the entrance, she moved out onto the street. As streams of light beamed down on her, joy swept through her like a wave, and she smiled without thinking.

Her hair, freshly washed after swimming that morning, was loose and she was wearing her favourite dress. It was the brightest blue she'd ever seen, with black stripes at the top and bottom. The material was so soft, she'd even thought about wearing it to bed, though her mum quickly put an end to that idea.

Running towards the Green, where the children gathered to play, the bottom of the dress ballooned like she was about to take off. And it felt like she could have too, if she'd wanted. Floated up high and looked down on everything. But right then, she wanted only to play.

Just before Nell reached the Green, the branches of a hedgerow sprang forward, stopping her in her tracks. Thwack! She ducked, and avoided them hitting her face, but they got her arms. The back of her head and dress were also hooked, caught within a twist of thorns. The pain was instant and not going away. She needed to get free.

Removing the tangles also hurt but Nell fought the pain, ducking down, low as can go, to move away from the hedge.

Suddenly she heard a rip – her dress! – and let out a cry. It was torn at the bottom on one side. There was laughter.

Confused, she looked up. Three girls, huddled together, stared back. All faces she knew but wearing a strange, shared expression. They must have been behind the hedge and jumped out.

Nell swallowed hard. The pain from the thorns had been overtaken by a sick feeling inside.

Chloe, the tallest girl, stepped forward.

'We set a trap for you. A Nell trap,' she said, her voice spiky with a face to match.

Nell shivered. Chloe and the space around her felt cold, even though it was a hot, hot day.

The other girls, Molly and Lily, giggled.

'We don't want to play with you anymore cos we don't like your frizz-ball hair or your poo-coloured face,' Chloe said, thrusting her face towards Nell's. 'Got that?'

Molly and Lily shrieked with laughter.

This wasn't the first time they'd ganged up on her, it'd been happening more and more, but nothing like this.

Nell looked at her torn dress then back at the smirking trio. Although a year younger than them, she was taller and stronger. She pictured herself picking them up, one by one, to send them flying across the Green. Like superheroes did to villains in the movies, with a crash landing. Surging forward, she grabbed hold of Chloe as Molly and Lily cried out then ran off.

Nell swept up the other girl, expecting a fight, but Chloe didn't move. The weight of her felt meringue light. When Nell met her eyes, the cold, taunting look had been replaced with bright, hot fear. Teasing, spiteful Chloe had vanished and switched places with a ragdoll. Nell let go and Chloe sunk down to the floor, sobbing. Leaving her there, Nell ran home faster than ever before.

Afterwards, the space in time between letting go of Chloe and landing face-down on her bed was a blur. Burying her head under her pillow, expecting the girls' parents to come knocking at the door, Nell remembered a cartoon. Its images flashed through her mind.

A monster had run away from its home – chased by an angry crowd of villagers.

'Monster!' 'You'll get what's coming to you! Monster!'

The villagers thought it'd hurt a child who'd been found injured.

Finally trapped and locked up in a cage, the monster looked out through the bars, its mouth flipped upside down with sadness. And the people pointed – large and lumpy with green skin, it must be bad.

But the cartoon had started with the monster saving the child. The villagers hadn't seen that.

When the child explained the monster had actually saved his life, they let it go. Everyone cheered this time and even the monster smiled. But the happy ending hadn't felt so happy to Nell because of the bits before. They'd all thought it was guilty because of the way it looked.

Chloe, Lily and Molly had made a trap for her. Like she was a monster.

And, she had actually done something. She'd grabbed hold of Chloe, meaning to do worse, and scared the other girls. It was wrong to hurt other people, her mum had taught her this.

But the girls, especially Chloe, had been mean to her first. And the more she thought about Chloe's words – and the girls' laughter - the more she hurt inside.

Nell's mum had hair and skin like the girls and her brother's skin was much lighter brown than hers. His curls were looser than hers too. She grabbed a handful of her hair in frustration. Why wasn't it smooth, why didn't it tumble downwards and shine in the light like everyone else's? She'd always liked the look of her brown skin but maybe they were right and it was wrong.

Nell hid the dress under her bed and changed into a plain t-shirt and shorts. Her nan had taught her how to sew and given her a sewing kit with needles, cottons and a pair of scissors. She could try and mend the tear. But when she eventually pulled the dress back out, she felt she didn't deserve it.

Making the tear bigger and bigger by pulling on it, she wanted to rip the dress up, but it stayed in one piece. Fishing the scissors out of her kit, she snipped at the dress - cut and cut – until she was left with just a pile of uneven pieces. A messy jigsaw of cotton scraps that she shoved back underneath the bed.

Nell spent the whole evening listening for the door, expecting the sound of furious banging, like the time she'd locked her brother outside on purpose. She was quiet, not even reacting when her brother gave her a flick at the dinner table. The sick feeling was still there.

'This isn't like you Nell,' her mum said, clearing away her barely touched plate. 'You must be coming down with something.'

Nell hadn't replied. She didn't want to open her mouth in case what happened came spilling out.

The next day, the weather was cloudy and dull. She skulked about the house, finding old toys, former favourites, to help fill the time. She rediscovered a puzzle of a duck family and a cloth cat she used to take everywhere, then moved them upstairs to her bedroom because her brother called them babyish. But they helped her forget and she breathed in the safe, bright surroundings of her home.

The following day, Nell looked out of a downstairs window and saw the sun had returned. And despite the sick feeling also having come back, she longed to be on the other side.

Before the end of the morning, there was a knock at the door. Not the pounding of angry fists Nell had been imagining, more a soft, hesitant tapping.

'Get the door, Nell. I'm right in the middle of something,' her mum shouted from the kitchen.

The front porch wasn't visible from the window, so Nell couldn't see who was standing there. She had no choice but to do as her mum said. Bracing herself for the worst, she opened the door just enough to peek outside. There on the step was Lily and Molly, the two girls that had run off when she'd turned on Chloe.

'Are you coming out to play?' Molly asked.

Nell checked both girl's faces, suspiciously.

Molly was beaming and Lily, holding out a skipping rope, also smiled widely.

'We can take it in turns to jump,' Lily said. 'We need three people to play.'

Nell glanced down the length of the garden path. The girls were definitely alone.

'Where's Chloe?' she asked.

Both girls shrugged.

'Not sure. Haven't seen Chloe,' Molly said, wrinkling her nose, like 'Chloe' had become a bad word.

Nell was confused. Both girls usually followed Chloe around. So much so she couldn't remember ever seeing them without her. But she wanted to believe Lily and Molly, because she really wanted to play.

'Ok,' she said, 'I'll just let my mum know.'

When they reached the Green, the two girls held the rope and insisted Nell jump first. She was half expecting it to be another trap but soon forgot herself and started singing her own, goofy versions of the skipping songs they all knew. Soon all three were in fits of giggles.

A little while later a figure approached the Green. It looked like Chloe, but she wasn't walking in her usual style, like she'd run you over if you were in her way. Nell looked again. It was

Chloe but she was hanging back, moving in slow-motion. The other two girls must have seen Chloe but ignored her. Eventually she arrived right in front of them, but no one said a word. Lily and Molly stared at the ground rather than at Chloe's face.

Nell looked warily at Chloe but saw right away she looked sorry. She was like a watered-down version of her usual self, and it didn't make Nell feel good. So, when Chloe gave her a lopsided, apologetic looking smile, Nell smiled back and motioned for her to join in. Soon they were all playing and laughing together as if nothing had ever happened.

And what had happened was never mentioned. It didn't take long for Chloe to regain her status as ringleader, only now Nell was number two, her sidekick. The summer went by, and the days passed in a happy haze. But sometimes when Nell was alone, the sick feeling came back.

When Nell's mum asked her where the dress was, she lied.

'Dunno. It must have got lost in the wash,' she said.

Her mum hadn't questioned her further, because things did get lost in the wash from time to time. But lying to her mum and thinking about her dress, in tatters under her bed, made her feel bad.

When Chloe failed to appear at the Green one morning, Nell, Molly and Lily went to her house, to find her. Chloe's mum had answered the door and shown them in.

'Here's the brave little warrior,' she said.

Chloe was sat on the sofa, her lower right arm wrapped in tea towels, the coffee table laden with sweets. She smirked at them and held the limb in the air.

'Bee sting,' Chloe said. 'It was the worst pain ever!'

The other girls gathered around her, gasping as she shifted the towels and a pack of ice to reveal her lower arm. It was bloated, almost square at the end like a boat paddle, with a raised angry lump where the sting had hit.

The worst pain ever.

'Hmm,' thought Nell.

Molly and Lily eyed Chloe in awe for the rest of the morning.

That night in bed, Nell thought about the day and how it had been all about Chloe and the bee sting. She considered how the other two girls had treated Chloe like she was some kind of hero. And that's when she had the idea.

The next day, she found a bee outside and followed it along a hedgerow, until it landed on a flower. Then Nell pressed it with her thumb, pushing it into the flower's yellow centre.

Sudden pain caused her to scream, and she ran back up her garden path towards home. Her eyes a stream of tears that didn't stop until back indoors and the pain started to lessen. The thumb was swollen, and her mum put a numbing ointment and bandage on the infected area.

She told her mum and brother that the bee had appeared out of nowhere and stung her.

'Bee stings are really dangerous! A boy in my class had to go to hospital when he got stung,' her brother said, his eyes widened then narrowed. 'And, that Bee will probably be dead now. Bees die when they use their sting.'

Nell hadn't known that. She ran upstairs to her bedroom, to cry again. Getting stung on purpose had been her worse idea ever. It was more dangerous than she'd imagined, and she'd also hurt a bee. Trying too hard to fit in had made her feel nearly as bad as feeling different had.

Seeing her friends at The Green later that day didn't make her feel any better.

'Woah, Nell!'

Molly and Lilly gasped and looked at her in awe, like when Chloe got stung. Chloe nodded and gave Nell a look, like they members of a secret club that the other two girls didn't know about. But Nell knew there wasn't a club really. She'd seen how quickly and easily things could change. It had felt nice to be in with Chloe that summer but now she felt something else. And it wasn't the good feeling she'd planned for.

So, at the end of her eighth summer, Nell decided to tell her mum the truth about her dress and what had happened with the girls. The pain from the bee sting had faded within hours, but the pain from earlier that summer – the girls setting a trap for her, Chloe's mean words and what happened straight afterwards – not so.

It felt that whilst some pain comes and goes, other pain can stay with you and feel heavy to carry around. Like rocks in your pocket or wellies full of water, but worse because it's inside. And then, there was pain that could go even deeper than that, that could hurt at the very core of you. And Nell wanted to get out what she'd been holding inside.

'Mum,' Nell said, one morning after breakfast. 'Do you remember when my dress went missing...'

Her mum was wiping the kitchen table with a dish cloth but put it down to turn and look at Nell.

'Yes?' The mention of the dress, its disappearance still a mystery, had grabbed her mum's attention.

Nell wasn't sure what her mum would do or say after she told her. It wasn't always easy to guess how adults might act. But she thought there might be something in accepting one type of pain, such as a telling off from her mum, if it meant another type could be avoided or lessened. Because she'd felt something far worse beyond that, a type of pain that could destroy her.